FIRES OF OUR CHOOSING

FIRES OF OUR CHOOSING

stories

Eugene Cross

1334 Woodbourne Street
Westland, MI 48186
www.dzancbooks.org

The characters and events in this book are fictitious. Any similarity to real persons, living or dead, is coincidental and not intended by the author.

FIRES OF OUR CHOOSING

Grateful acknowledgment is made to the following publications, in which these stories first appeared, often in different forms:

"Rosaleen, If You Know What I Mean," *American Short Fiction*; "Passengers," *Storyglossia*; "Harvesters," and "The Brother," *Narrative Magazine*; "Hunters," *Hobart*; "This Too," *TriQuarterly*; "Fires of Our Choosing," *Story Quarterly;* "Come August," *The Pinch*; "Only the Strong Will Survive," *Third Coast;* "The Gambler," *New South*; "430," *Freight Stories*; "Eyes Closed," *Callaloo & Texas Told'em: Gambling Stories*

Published 2012 by Dzanc Books
Book design by Steven Seighman

ISBN: 978-1-936-87307-4
First edition: March 2012

This project is supported in part by an award from the National Endowment for the Arts.

Printed in the United States of America

10 9 8 7 6 5 4 3 2

CONTENTS

In memory of my father,
who always believed.

Eugene Charles Cross
(1936-2005)

FIRES OF OUR CHOOSING

Rosaleen, If You Know What I Mean

THE DAY AFTER his brother left the house for good, Marty Hanson picked out the smallest boy in his sixth grade class and waited until the boy was alone. He approached him, telling him that he'd found a dead dog decomposing in a far corner of the school's courtyard. The boy, who was new at the school and whose name Marty could not remember, stuffed his hands deep into his pockets, nearly to the elbows, and said, "So?" He was looking at a dandelion near his sneaker's toe.

"'So?'" Marty said, staring at the boy. "*So* I dare you to come over and have a look."

The boy kept his eyes trained on the ground, his head tilted forward. Marty saw the cowlick in the boy's hair. Probably that morning his mother had tried to comb it down with a wet brush, Marty thought.

"I knew you were a pussy. Jimmy Dinuzio told me so." Marty had seen the two hanging around.

"Jimmy didn't say that."

"Whatever," Marty said. He began to turn away. Before he'd taken two full steps he heard the boy say, "Where is it?"

Marty led him to the southeast corner of the courtyard where two evergreens stood like sentries. He pointed to the base of one of the trees where the branches hung low and bare and darkened the ground. Dry pine needles were scattered everywhere.

"Over there," Marty said. The boy walked slowly, waving his hand in front of him as though he was blind. Marty followed close behind, and by the time the boy realized there was no dog, it was too late, Marty already had him on the ground. He straddled his chest and pounded his head and torso with his fists. He had trapped one of the boy's hands with his knee, and when the boy tried to shield his face with the other, Marty tore it away. He dropped his bony elbows onto the boy's chest and ribs and he spit on him until his mouth went dry. The boy's screams sounded to Marty like a car peeling out, like the high-pitched squeal of rubber on asphalt.

Marty had picked the spot by the evergreens in part because of its distance from Ms. Neppick, the recess proctor that week. By the time she arrived, the boy's screaming had withered down to quiet sobs, more a gasping for air and heaving of the chest than anything. After she pulled Marty off, grabbing him with both hands by his hair and yanking him to the side, he lay in the grass panting as she said the boy's name over and over. Marty stared at the cloudless sky and felt such a relief that he began to repeat it too. "Joshua," he said. "*Joshua, Joshua, Joshua.*"

From the room where he was being kept, Marty could see the flashing red lights of the ambulance as it pulled up. A woman paramedic emerged from the driver's side. She swung open the back doors like a gate and a fat man in shorts stepped out. He was carrying a black bag and had a walkie-talkie hanging from his belt. Marty watched the two of them jog into the building. At the front of the room, the school's custodian, Phil, stood in front of the closed door. He was a wiry man with long veins that ran down his arms and into his hands. He was staring at Marty, shaking his head every now and again. When Marty looked up at him, Phil said, "A million other things I could be doing."

Marty looked at his hands. The blood on his knuckles was beginning to dry. He rubbed at them with his thumb until the wounds began to seep.

"What makes you so special?" Phil suddenly asked. He was standing directly in front of Marty's desk, though Marty hadn't noticed him walking over.

"I don't know what you mean," Marty said.

"Yes, you damn well do," Phil said. He took one of his big veiny hands, made a fist, and brought it down hard on the center of the desk. Marty didn't flinch but noticed the bottom half of a tattoo sticking out from Phil's shirt sleeve. A dragon's tail, Marty thought, or a woman's name written in big looping cursive. Phil saw him looking, ran his fingertips over the design, and smiled. "Oh well," he said, "just thought I'd see how it felt." He turned and walked back to his post by the door. "Give me the boiler room any day."

Joshua, the boy Marty had hurt, was kept overnight at the hospital for observation. One of his eyes had swollen shut and one rib had cracked. A plastic surgeon sewed several stitches near his lip using a suture so thin it became invisible when held up to light.

As part of his punishment, in addition to being expelled, Marty was to visit Joshua at home and offer an apology should he ever express a desire to hear it. It seemed he never would. Since the summer had almost arrived, Marty's mother deferred enrolling him in a different school until the fall and instead sent him twice a week to the anger counseling sessions the juvenile judge had ordered. When she dropped him off at the first Tuesday night session she did not turn to look at him.

"I'll be back at eight," she said, staring at the gear shift. She looked exhausted, her eyes as dull and frosted-over as sea glass. The previous August, Marty's father had been out jogging along his usual route when a car travelling eastbound slipped off the shoulder of the road and struck and killed him. The car did not stop, nor was there any indication that it had slowed. Marty's father's body was thrown several dozen feet through the air before it came to rest among a tangle of undergrowth and litter.

Marty had been at summer camp and did not find out till later that day. He was returning from a nature walk, and deep in his pocket was a turtle shell covered in intricate swirls that he'd taken from near the swamp when no one was looking. Marty wanted to show the shell to his brother, Nate. He wanted to ask Nate about the turtle that had carried the shell on its back to see if he had an answer as to what had happened to it. They were not supposed to take anything they found on the nature walk and, for one brief moment, when Marty emerged from the trailhead and saw Nate standing beside a state trooper near the camp's office, he thought he'd been caught.

"Thanks for the ride," Marty said, stepping out onto the sidewalk. His mother nodded and he shut the door being careful not to slam it.

The anger management sessions were held in a church basement, a long narrow room with columns supporting a low water-stained ceiling. At one end was a stage with a wooden podium and a large steel bingo cage. Folding tables and chairs were stacked against the walls and a line of windows near the ceiling looked out at the parking lot. The room smelled like a mixture of smoke and Play-Doh. Marty sat on one of the plastic chairs that had been arranged in a circle near the center of the room. A skinny boy with bug eyes sat down beside him.

"What are you in for?" he asked.

Marty hesitated for a few moments and then said, "Fighting."

"Wow," the boy said, "fighting." He turned to an older boy who was sitting next to him. "Hey, Rodney, this kid's in for fighting. Wow, huh?" The bug-eyed boy turned back to Marty and stuck out his tongue, his mouth stretched open like a cave. His breath was warm and sour. He kept his tongue out until Marty noticed that he'd written *Get Fukd* on it in green ink.

The session counselor, Ms. Higgins, reminded Marty of a catfish. She was heavyset with a sparse black mustache above a thin set of lips. She wore a flowing muumuu covered in a tropical design and a big turquoise medallion on a chain around her neck. She began by making each person stand and offer an introduction. Besides Marty there were seven others, most of them older, all of them boys except for one girl who sat directly across from him. The girl had close-cropped hair that she'd bleached the color out of. It looked to Marty as though her skull was showing through, and he wondered if that was the effect she'd intended. Marty waited while the others stood. Some of them introduced themselves with an annoyed tone as though speaking to a younger sibling. Others spoke with their heads down, chins glued to their chests. Most of them had been there before and seemed familiar with each other. When it was Marty's turn to stand, the bug-eyed boy said, "He's in here for fighting. Can you believe it?"

"Quiet, Elliot," Ms. Higgins said, "or I'll place a call to your father." The boy's head dropped.

"Go on, Marty," Ms. Higgins said. Marty gave the information she had asked for. He was twelve years old. He liked dessert pizza and swimming. He had a hamster named Lebron James. He could not remember what he'd dreamed last.

For their first exercise they were split up in pairs. Marty was partnered with the girl, whose name was Clairie. They had been instructed to share the one thing of which they were most proud. Marty was having trouble coming up with something. For a long time neither of them spoke.

"I taught my hamster to fetch," he finally said. It was true. Using peanuts and raisins, he'd trained Lebron to retrieve a ping-pong ball and roll it to the cage door. After a moment, Clairie began to nod very slowly as though she was beginning to understand how this could be a point of pride for someone. She had green eyes. Two moles near her eyebrow sat one above the other like a colon.

"I heard people put those up their asses," she said, still nodding.

"Put what up their asses?" Marty asked.

"Hamsters. I read it online." For one terrifying moment, Marty envisioned Lebron James skittering around inside his body, clawing at his organs, his light beige fur soaked in blood.

"That's impossible," he said. Clairie shrugged her shoulders.

"If you can teach them to fetch," she said, "it seems to me anything's possible."

For a long time, Marty wondered what he'd been doing at the exact moment his father had died. Earlier that day there had been a craft session, and so it was possible that at the precise instant the car struck his father, Marty had been gluing elbow macaroni to construction paper. After craft the campers went swimming in the lake, and so it was also possible that as Marty's father drew his last breath, Marty was underwater holding his own, or playing Marco Polo or squishing his toes as deep as he could into the muddy floor of the lake. There was a heavy boy at the camp who kept his shirt on when he swam. The other boys simply called him Tits, but Marty never did, except for one time, the day his father died. And so it was also possible, Marty realized, that in the split second it took for his father to go from running to flying, in his last moment on this earth, Marty had been doing something bad.

From the kitchen table, Marty watched his mother prepare dinner. She moved slowly along the length of the counter: slicing bread, boiling pasta, running a jar of sauce under hot water. It had been a month since the incident at school, and his mother rarely spoke of it. Occasionally she asked how the sessions with Ms. Higgins were going, but Marty knew she wanted only simple answers, nothing that would require a follow-up question, and so he provided only those.

Nine months after her husband's death, she still spent much of her time behind her bedroom door. She had not returned to work, and so her days drifted along without event, anchored only by those times when she had to drop Marty off at school or pick him up. Since his expulsion, there was not even that. Meals were eaten in front of the TV with the sound turned low, Vanna White floating back and forth across the screen as though observing them. At some point his mother had begun cleaning almost religiously. Everything had its own particular place, and if the order was in any way upset, she'd simply return the object without comment. The house began to feel like a department store, everything meticulously arranged, his mother staring through the bay windows in the darkened living room as still as a mannequin.

He knew these were the reasons Nate had left, the endless quiet making even the air seem stale. He'd moved to North Carolina with friends, his plans shifting and vague. He said he would work at the beach, go back to college, take up a trade. He had left early, before Marty woke for school. Marty had never shown him the turtle shell, and now it was too late.

He watched his mother dump the pasta into a strainer, a cloud of steam rising past her face. Her light brown hair was pulled back in a ponytail, and a loose strand stuck to her damp neck. She'd lost weight, even more since Nate had gone, and Marty saw the sharp cuts of her shoulder blades through her blouse. "Do you need any help?" he asked. It was beginning to rain, and fat drops streaked the window above the sink. His mother transferred the pasta to a serving bowl and dumped the jar of sauce over top. If she'd heard him ask, she didn't let on.

Lying in bed, Marty watched Lebron James run in his wheel, spinning it so fast it hummed. Ms. Higgins had given them homework although not the kind you brought in. She had instructed them to begin thinking about why they were there. Eventually, she said, they would need to come to a *reckoning* with what they had done. Marty did not know what this word meant; he'd been too embarrassed to ask. He thought of Joshua, the way his body had felt pinned beneath his own, thin and frail like something only partly there. He wondered if Joshua's rib had healed, if his eye had reopened. He wondered if he would ever call to tell Marty he was ready for his apology. Lebron jumped off his wheel. His nails clacked against the plastic of his water bottle. Marty imagined Nate renting jet skis to tourists with sunburns and fanny packs. He saw him sitting in a classroom copying notes from the board. He had not called since he'd left, and for a moment Marty hoped that wherever he was, he was not happy. Marty leaned over and switched off his bedside lamp. Lebron squeaked at the sudden darkness and clawed at his cage. "Reckoning," Marty said, the sound of it out loud scaring him.

"Do not remove your blindfold," Ms. Higgins said. The exercise was called Minefield and was simple enough. One partner led the other through a series of obstacles, mostly scattered couch cushions and overturned chairs. The one who was blindfolded had to trust his partner's directions. Marty could feel his muscles constrict as he waited for Clairie to tell him what to do next. He had been relieved when Ms. Higgins had paired them up again. He still had no idea what Clairie had done to be among them, but he was thankful he had not been partnered with Elliot, who mocked him endlessly, or Rodney, who he'd heard was attending the sessions for having kicked a dog to death in a friend's basement.

"Two steps forward," Clairie whispered as though it was a secret. "Small ones." Marty stretched his foot out cautiously, tracing the linoleum with the toe of his Nike. He felt his body trying to balance itself. "You're supposed to trust me," Clairie said. "You're not even trying."

"I don't even know you," Marty said. He wasn't sure if Clairie was still standing beside him or if she'd moved. He was aware of his breathing and tried slowing it. He wanted to rip off the blindfold, and had to concentrate hard to keep his hands at his sides.

"I think that's the point." Clairie's voice came from somewhere in front of him. Occasionally, he heard other guides offer their partners directions, but still, he imagined everyone with their blindfolds off, circled around him, even Ms. Higgins, stifling giggles as he stumbled forward an inch at a time. Or worse, he imagined that they'd all left, that he was standing in the church basement alone. If he removed his blindfold he'd find that the last person out had killed the lights, plunging the room into the same darkness he was experiencing now.

"What next?" Marty asked, though he still hadn't taken a full step. When Clairie didn't answer, he lifted his arm to the side and brought it around in a long slow wave as though silencing an orchestra.

"Marty." Clairie was standing directly behind him. Ms. Higgins's voice came from a distance as she congratulated a pair somewhere across the room. Clairie traced a finger down the bumpy nodules of his spine and he shivered. "I know why you're *really* here," she said. She ran her nails along the hem of one T-shirt sleeve. "My friend's younger brother goes to Jefferson and told me all about it. I wouldn't call that fighting." She rested her fingertips on his triceps. He felt the moisture of her breath on the back of his neck. "That was some brutal shit," she whispered.

She pinched a section of skin overtop the muscle and squeezed hard. It burned, and he remembered the way Joshua's lip had opened suddenly, the flesh splitting to reveal the brightness of blood. Marty clenched his teeth and tried to remain perfectly still. "Kind of hot if you ask me," she said, "giving some helpless kid a beatdown for no reason." He could feel her lips forming the words near the edge of his ear. He tried to concentrate on her voice but she pinched him harder. White flashes filled his vision. "You're a real brute," she said, digging her fingernails deeper. Tears formed in the corners of his eyes and soaked into the blindfold. Finally, she released his skin, the burn that remained nearly as bad. "Now move the fuck forward." Marty raised his foot and took a step.

A few days later, Joshua's mother called for the apology. She wanted to set up a face-to-face meeting. She asked Marty's mother to bring him into the room while they spoke and to place her on speaker-phone. They did not have speaker-phone, so Marty sat beside his mother on the couch while she held the receiver between their ears. Joshua's mother used terms like "healing process" and "closure." She sounded oddly cheerful, but her words were muffled and hard to make out as though she herself was on speaker-phone. Marty wondered if Joshua was sitting beside her, if she had her arm around his shoulders for encouragement. "This is just another step," she said.

Marty's mother apologized again as she had at the school disciplinary hearing and his juvenile court date. "There have been some difficulties lately," she added.

"We are all evolving," Joshua's mother said, "each and every one of us. There's no need to retread old ground, Rosaleen."

Marty felt a pit open in his stomach. He had not heard his mother called by her name in a long time. He looked toward the front door and remembered his dad coming in from a jog, his round face flushed, crescents of sweat beneath each arm. He would stretch his calves by leaning forward and pushing against the wall as though he meant to topple it. He had a way of play-rhyming his wife's name. "Rosaleen and her magic spleen," he would sing loudly, trying to draw her out from wherever she was in the house. He would walk into the kitchen, stopping to drink straight from the faucet, and then move room to room looking for her. Marty and Nate would trail him as he opened and closed doors, tapping his fingertips against the drywall, calling out his nonsense rhymes. "Rosaleen owns a crystal canteen. Rosaleen, let's get

PG-13." When he finally found her, she would squeal and laugh as he chased her down, wrapping her in his sweaty arms and saying over and over, "Rosaleen, if you know what I mean."

Marty reached up and pressed on the bruise Clairie had left. At first there had been only some redness and two curved marks like parentheses where her nails had broken the skin, but now a green and purple bruise, yellowed at its center, covered an area the size of a half-dollar.

"Saturday for lunch then," Joshua's mother was saying. "Why don't you bring him by around eleven? And we'd love it if you could stay as well. Are there any dietary restrictions?" Marty's mother twisted the phone cord around her fingers like a rosary.

"No," she said, "none that I can think of."

The Reserve was a new wooded subdivision near the edge of the city. The development bordered a golf course and several of the striking green fairways wound their way past the homes. Many of the lots were still being leveled and huge backhoes and graders sat on wide tracts of fresh dirt. Most of the houses were two-story brick structures with copper overhangs and multi-tiered roofs that slanted down at dramatic angles. None of the lawns had grass and the houses rose from the middle of the bare yards as though they'd sprung directly from the earth. Marty sat staring up at Joshua's house, which looked like all the others. Deep in his pocket was the turtle shell. He'd retrieved it the night before from the shoebox beneath his bed, which also contained two M-80s, a Zippo lighter he'd found in the mall parking lot, a *Frederick's of Hollywood* catalogue he'd swiped from Nate's room, and the Swiss Army knife his father had secretly given him for his eleventh birthday, a gift his mother would have deemed too dangerous. She sat in the driver's seat wearing a blue patterned sundress, both hands gripping the wheel. They were in the driveway, but she had yet to put the car in park. By the time she turned to him, Marty already knew what she was going to say.

"I don't think I'll be able to make it." Marty felt his cheeks burn. It was the same thing she'd said before his club-team soccer playoffs, the same vague excuse she'd offered for missing his school's parent-teacher conferences. "Here," she said, handing him her cell phone. "You can call me at the house when you're ready to get picked up." A golf green sat at a distance and Marty watched a man line up a putt. He struck it and then squatted low, waving his arm frantically as though directing the ball. Marty couldn't stop the tears and so he turned toward his window. He wished he'd stolen the blindfold from the Minefield exercise. He wished he were wearing it now.

"But you *promised* her." He spoke slowly to keep his voice from breaking, feeling each word. "They're expecting you." His hands were at his sides, and he felt the rough ridge of the turtle shell through his khaki shorts.

"I didn't *promise*," she said. "I did not." If Nate had been there, he would have fought with her, accused her until she herself was in tears. They were brothers, but they had always been different that way.

Marty took hold of the door handle. He lifted his shoulder and rubbed his eyes across it roughly. "Please don't make me go alone." He hated the way it sounded, regretted it the second it came out. He saw himself as Nate might, whiny and weak. He was the real pussy and that was why Nate hadn't called. Before she had time to respond, he pushed open the door and jumped out.

Joshua's mother answered the door wearing a ruffled skirt fastened with a braided leather belt, a frilly top the color of freshly tilled soil, and earrings that looked to Marty like miniature wind chimes. A bright raspberry headscarf came halfway down her tan forehead and held back her dark blond hair. "Won't your mother be joining us?" she asked, looking out over Marty's head as though she might be hiding somewhere.

"She's not feeling so well," Marty said. "Allergies." He was having trouble looking at her when he spoke.

"I'm sorry to hear that." She smiled, trying to hide her disappointment, then invited him in. "You should tell her to try tea tree oil," she said, shutting the door behind him. "I spritz the entire house with it."

She led Marty through a series of bright rooms, each painted the color of a different fruit: lime green, tangerine orange, cherry red. The place had not been completely settled into. Unpacked boxes were stacked in corners and modern-looking furniture and exotic artwork were scattered about the house in no discernible order. Three giraffes with their necks intertwined, carved from a single piece of wood nearly as tall as him, stood near a hallway closet; the dining room table was covered with African tribal masks; a Navajo rug resting against a wall had begun to unroll like a giant, elaborately patterned tongue. In the living room, floor to ceiling windows looked out on a sloping dirt yard that ran to the edge of a lush green fairway. A stone path cut the yard in half. A wide hole had been dug for a pond and was draped in a shiny black liner and surrounded by colorful rocks. In the center of the room, the coffee table was hidden beneath a stack of blueprints.

"Joshua's father is an eco-architect," she said when she noticed Marty looking. "We moved here when the city hired him as a consultant. Unfortunately, he's working so he won't be able to join us." She led Marty to the top of a stairwell. "Joshua's playing downstairs," she said. "I'll give you two some time alone before lunch." She began to turn and then hesitated. The look on her face seemed to indicate that she was arguing some point with herself. Marty buried his hands deep into his pockets. He hunched his shoulders and kept his eyes trained on a section of the tile floor where the grout had begun to chip away. "You know why you're here, right?" she asked. Marty could feel her staring at him. He nodded slightly.

"To apologize," he said.

"To explain…" she began to say and then stopped herself. Marty could feel her choosing her words. "I'm a firm believer in forgiveness. I think we all need this, that it will be beneficial and healing for all of us, you included. But you have to understand, Joshua is our only child and when I answered the phone that day…" Marty could hear her voice begin to falter like a radio station losing its signal. "Do you have any siblings, or is it just you?" Marty dug his fingernails into the palms of his hands. Joshua's mother was wearing strappy sandals and he noticed that she'd painted the toenails of one foot a different color than thc other. He wanted to ask her why she'd done this, what it meant.

"It's just me," he said.

Joshua sat on the carpeted floor of the basement playing a video game that required him to wear a headset. He had yet to acknowledge Marty, who was sitting in an overstuffed easy chair on the other side of the room, his legs crossed beneath him. Marty watched the screen as Joshua lined up a Nazi in the crosshairs of his sniper rifle. He hit a button on his controller, and the Nazi flailed wildly, a spray of red escaping his head before he collapsed to the ground.

"My mom's making me do this," Joshua said without looking over. "I asked to take karate lessons, and she said I couldn't until I did this." He laid the video game controller on the carpet and stood. He looked bigger than Marty remembered, taller at least, and he seemed weighted down on one side, slightly unlevel as though one leg was longer than the other. Marty hoped he had not somehow done this to him. Joshua wore cargo shorts and a T-shirt advertising the Outer Banks. His hair had been cut short for the summer, and the cowlick was gone.

"She's a nice lady," Marty said.

"She's a lot nicer than my dad would have been to you." Joshua curled his bare toes and pressed them against the carpet, making hollow popping sounds. "He never works on Saturdays. He just didn't want to be here for this. He said he didn't agree with it." Joshua walked over to a pinball machine that stood in the corner. He pulled back the plunger and released it. A row of lights flashed along the top. "He said he didn't want you in our house." Marty heard Joshua's mother moving somewhere above them. He wondered what she was doing, what color room she was in. He suddenly wanted to be upstairs with her, listening as she explained her husband's work, or helping her prepare lunch. Joshua clicked the machine's levers, though he didn't seem to be paying much attention to the game.

"You jumped me," he said. "That's all you did. You tricked me, and then you jumped me." He walked over to where Marty sat. "You lied to me about Jimmy and I believed you." Joshua's face was skinny and tanned. The marks on it had healed. Marty wondered if there was a bump on his lip where the stitches had been. A spray of freckles formed a band over the bridge of his nose. Joshua shook his head as though disappointed with himself. His eyes were deep brown and wild in his head. "This never would have happened if we had stayed in Charlotte. I had a million friends back home," he said. He looked at the stairwell and then back at Marty. "My mom told my dad what happened, right in front of the doctor. She said *assaulted* but everyone knows that means beat up." Without warning Joshua reached into his pocket and took out a heavy black gun. He straightened his arm and aimed it directly at Marty's eye. Marty edged his body back against the chair.

"I could kill you right now, and nobody would blame me." His arm was unsteady and the gun wavered at the end of it. Marty pressed further back into the chair. He wanted to yell for Joshua's mother, but he could not open his mouth. He squeezed his eyes shut and tried to imagine himself anywhere else. In the church basement with Ms. Higgins, Clairie standing behind him telling him what to do, calling him a brute. In his room listening to Lebron James spin his wheel into a hum. He tried to picture his mother. What would she be doing right then, at the exact moment he died? Watching TV on mute, vacuuming the den for the third time that day? He thought of how she missed his dad, how she missed Nate. For a moment he hoped Joshua would do it.

"You picked me because I was new," Joshua said. Marty shook his head.

"Because you were the smallest."

"Does that make you better or something?" Joshua asked.

"No," Marty said. "I just want to tell the truth." A chrome cylinder extended from the handle of the gun. Joshua noticed Marty looking at it.

"This is a high-powered CO2 air pistol," he said.

"Does that mean BB gun?" Marty asked.

"It *means* I could shoot you right now and it would

probably kill you. At the very least your eye would explode into a giant blob of shit and then you'd be half-blind. How would you like that?" Joshua's voice cracked and he pressed the cold end of the gun into Marty's skin. He pushed harder, forcing Marty's head into the back of the chair. The metal of the gun rubbed against his cheekbone.

"My brother moved to North Carolina," Marty said.

"I wish I still lived there. I hate this place." Joshua took the gun out of Marty's cheek. "What city did he move to?"

"I don't know," Marty said. "He left before I woke up." Marty was still pressed into a corner of the chair. The turtle shell dug into the fleshy part of his thigh. He realized he was crying, silently, hot tears sliding along the crease of his nose. Joshua had lowered the gun and was staring at him. He looked confused. From the top of the stairs his mother called that it was time to eat.

"Your brother *moved* and he didn't tell you *where*?"

Marty shook his head. Joshua looked at him and then placed the gun back into his pocket.

"*He* probably hates you too."

For lunch they had couscous and grilled vegetables. The three of them ate at the kitchen counter, Joshua's mother doing most of the talking. When they had almost finished, Marty asked to use the bathroom. He walked past where Joshua's mother directed him and slid out the mudroom door. Once outside, he placed the turtle shell beside a soccer ball where he hoped Joshua would find it. Then he cut through the side yard and across the road. He walked along the shoulder for a short while and then ducked into some woods. He heard a creek running somewhere and followed the sound, stepping over undergrowth and fallen trees until he found it moving quickly in the shade. He could see all the way down to the slate bottom. He chose a smooth log on the bank and sat against it. The air was hot, and he lowered his feet into the cool water, sneakers and all. Everything seemed lighter somehow. Minnows flashed silver in the shallows. The sun coming down through the leaves made tiny white ovals of light on the surface of the water. He wondered if this was how Nate had felt riding in his friend's car that morning, every truck stop and exit sign taking him farther away. His mother's cell phone was still in his pocket and he did not want to hear it ring. He did not want to go home. If she called he might ignore it or throw it into the fast moving water of the creek. Or he might answer the call and press the tiny device to his ear. "What is happening?" she might say, her voice barely controlled, wonderfully urgent. "Where are you?" He pictured her searching for him frantically, scouring Joshua's neighborhood, calling the police. The thought raised his skin and made him shiver.

She had let him believe she'd come with him to Joshua's, and then she'd made him go alone. He could lie to her too. He could say anything he wanted. "I'm still here," he might tell her, the water rushing over his ankles, the slickness of the log working itself against his back. "I never left."

Passengers

SHE IS TALKING ABOUT her father again, and I don't mind listening. Her stories are usually more interesting than mine and I like her voice, the way it fills a place. We are in my car. I guess we're parking, if that's what you'd call it, although we aren't in the back seat and all of our clothes are intact. We are down at the Peninsula, off on the bay side next to a thin stretch of beach. I know about the spot from sailing. My father showed it to me once when I was younger and we used to take the boat out together. Across the bay I can see downtown Erie, the lights of the bars and restaurants as bright as bonfires. Outside it is hot, with just a little bit of a breeze coming in off the water. We are the only two around.

She tells me again how her father, when he was younger, had a wild streak in him. She tells me about the parties he threw, complete with gin baths and people jumping off the roof naked into the swimming pool and white lines from one side of the kitchen counter to the other. She has heard all this secondhand from her father's friends. But after she was born, he finally got himself straightened out.

I don't know exactly what to think of her father. I've never met him because by the time she and I got things going she was already living on her own, working long hours, paying her own bills. And by then they didn't speak anymore. I was getting the impression that that was basically where all of this was headed. Things had just fallen apart between the two of them.

She begins telling me about growing up. Most of it I already know. He raised her alone. When she was four, her mother ran off to Florida with a welterweight boxer and so it was just her and her dad.

"Through all of it," she says: the skinned knees, her first period, the heartbreaks. It was just him and her and so they had this special relationship. "But the fighting was always there," she says. "We fought, but at least back then we still talked." She slides closer to me on the leather seat. She is wearing a tank top, and her skin, where it touches my arm, feels hot and angry, like just talking about her father heats her blood. I free my arm from where it is wedged between us and stretch it across her shoulders. In front of us Presque Isle Bay is as shiny black as an oil slick. The lights of the Bicentennial Tower shiver on its surface.

"He's unreasonable," she says. "You're lucky you've never had to meet him." I nod, but not too dramatically. She can still get defensive about him.

With all the things she's told me, I shouldn't even want to meet him. According to her he's rash and bullheaded, can blow a fuse over the slightest thing. But still I'm curious. It's been half a year, and I haven't met any of her family, not a cousin or a grandparent. I have already introduced her to all of mine.

"I'm the one you're with," she says when we talk about it. "Those other people shouldn't matter."

My mother has a different opinion. She did some asking around and found out where the girl lived, and that was enough for her.

"Her stock is below yours," my mother told me one night several weeks after we began dating. We had just finished eating dinner and were sitting in the living room. My father was reading the paper, but when my mother said that he lowered it and looked over.

"I'm sure she's a nice girl, and I know you don't want to admit it now, but you'll never survive it." She spoke so matter-of-factly, like I was trying to change something I had no control over and she already knew how it would all end.

"We're in love, and that should be enough," I said, realizing immediately how childish I sounded. My mother looked at me in a sort of disappointed way.

"Take 'should be' to the bank," she said, "and tell me what you get for it."

Of course I never told her what my mother said. And to her face my mother acted pleasantly uninterested, the same way she treated my friends whose last names she did not recognize. When I brought her along to dinners my mother engaged her in brief conversations before turning away.

"Another thing about my father," she continues, "is that everything has to be taken to the extreme with him. He either loves you or he hates you, and sometimes one is as bad as the other." She stops and looks at me. Her face is round and seems to give off a pale glow. In the dark she always looks sad, even when I know she isn't.

"He never even laid eyes on me until I was three years old," she says. I have heard this before. She has told me he was in jail, during her birth, her first steps. She has told me her mother would not take her to visit him in prison. She has told me this much, but never goes any further. Like all the people she knows whom I've never met, may never meet, the rest is just speculation for me. "I told you he was in jail."

I nod, stare ahead at the bay, pretend to absorb this information without any questions, hoping she'll go on. I'm afraid to prompt or push her in any way, afraid that if I do, she'll abandon it, leaving me guessing. And besides that, it is her story to tell. But I have already wondered for a long time.

I lift my arm off her shoulders and over her head. I reach for her hand and grip it. It is almost the end of August and soon I'll be leaving for school. Leaving her here, to work and live the way she's done since long before meeting me. She knows this but doesn't like to talk about it. I feel like this is the closest I've come to really knowing her. Across the water Erie seems a thousand miles away. The distance makes me feel safe. "We're alone," I say. "Nothing can touch us here." And then with her hand warm and slick in mine and her head resting like a stone in the crook of my neck she tells her story.

"My father's brother, my Uncle Charlie, was his best friend growing up. They were only two years apart, so they played together, went to school together, everything. When my dad graduated from high school, Charlie was already working tool-and-die and so he got my dad a job at the same shop. It was alright at first, paid okay, but what they really wanted was to get into business for themselves, and both of them had done some construction in the past. So after saving for a while they found a rundown building on East 14th and Parade and bought it, cheap. They both still had their regular jobs, but on nights and weekends, they would go over there and work on it together, fixing it up. It took them some time but they turned the place into three separate apartments. Nothing fancy, but nice enough to rent. It was the first thing they ever really owned, and my dad still gets proud when he talks about it. So eventually they started to rent them out, but you know that area. Lots of crime. No one has a job. So of course they're getting stiffed on payments left and right. Tenants are staying for a few months, tearing the places apart partying, and then leaving. It gets to the point where my dad and Charlie have to start hounding people to get them to pay. But there's this one guy in particular. He hasn't paid rent since the first month, and he's almost never there so it's near impossible to even ask him about it. My dad and uncle are counting on this money; they only have the three units and they over-extended themselves. They have bills and credit lines, and my dad's got my mother at home pregnant with me. Things are about as tight as they can get. So one Saturday my dad and Charlie are over there replacing some siding, and they see the guy pull up. He parks across the street and half-stumbles out of the car like he's just getting home from drinking all night. Charlie is a little more laid back than my father, so he says to stay put and that he'll go talk to the guy and figure this out once and for all. So my dad keeps working and Charlie goes across the street to where the guy is. My dad can see them talking but he can't hear anything they're saying. It looks like they're arguing, but he can't tell for sure. Charlie says something else, and points at the building and the guy nods. Charlie starts walking back over to where my father is. He's got a big smile on his face like him and the guy have come to some agreement. My dad's just standing there watching, and he sees the guy reaching into the backseat for something. And then as calm as if he were unloading groceries the guy takes out a shotgun. My dad starts yelling and pointing, and Charlie turns around. But before he can do anything the guy shoots him in the stomach. Charlie gets knocked backwards on the pavement. Then the guy aims at my dad and shoots again. But he's too far and misses. The shotgun's no good from there. So he drops it and starts running, runs right past the wide open door of his car. Doesn't even think to jump in and drive off. And my dad's seeing all of this happen. His first instinct is to chase the guy, and so he starts running after him. By now people have come out on their porches but my dad doesn't see any of it. All he can think about is the guy. He already had a head start when my dad started chasing him, but it doesn't matter, all that matters to my dad is catching up with him. They run for blocks, dodging cars, cutting across lawns, my dad gaining ground little by little. And the whole time he's been chasing the guy, he's been holding the hammer he was working with. He hasn't even thought to drop it. When he finally catches up with the guy he reaches out and grabs a handful of his shirt and the two of them go down on the pavement in a ball. And my dad ends up on top, and the next thing he knows he's swinging, hitting the man full force with the hammer. He's hitting the guy everywhere, his chest, his arms, his head, and he keeps hitting until finally the guy stops moving, stops kicking and squirming and screaming beneath him. My dad stands up, walks over to the curb, and sits down. And that's how he stayed, covered in blood, still holding the hammer, until the police got there and arrested him. Charlie died in the ambulance on the way to the hospital, but not the other guy. After all that he lived, but it wasn't much of a life. He was at St. Mary's. He couldn't talk. He couldn't walk. For all practical purposes he was already dead. And normally, for something like that, my father could have been put away for life. But under the circumstances the jury knew he'd pretty much gone insane for a while. So he spent a little over three years in jail. And he hardly ever talks about it, but when he does he says he knows he did the right thing because he loved Charlie."

She stops and looks at me. I know she expects to see shock, and even though I try, how can I hide it? I can see my reaction through hers. There is a faint glow of light coming through the windshield, and I can see her expression. It is part pain, part indignation, like I am unjustly condemning her for something her father did years ago. But I can't help it. I am shocked. I have had a long time to guess at crimes her father may have committed and nothing like this crossed my mind. For a long time we sit silently. She leans away from me and takes her hand back from where it sits in my open palm. I let her story play itself out in my mind, watch as her father commits his crime, and then waits for the police, bloodied and tired. But there is something else that is bothering me. Another part of the story that will not settle.

"What about Charlie?" I ask.

She looks confused. "I told you. He died." There is resentment in her tone, as if she is angered by my asking about a man neither of us will ever meet.

"I know that. But why didn't your father stay with him, why didn't he go to him first?" I ask her. I can't help it. For some reason the question seems important. She pretends to look surprised, but she is smart and I know that these are questions she must have asked herself, although maybe she has not thought of them for a long time.

"I don't know," she says. "His first instinct was to chase the guy. He didn't even have time to think. It's easy to dissect it once it's over." Her voice is stern and I think about letting up, but I am angry. She defends her father like a child in a playground argument. I think about the things my mother said, and how I refuse to believe them, how I wouldn't just blindly defend someone because we shared the same blood.

"Maybe he thought Charlie was already dead." She is scrambling now, making excuses for a man she no longer talks to. And I'm not buying any of it.

"But wouldn't he at least check? Wouldn't he go over there and check?"

"You don't understand," she says. "I thought you would, but you don't." Her words are flat and deliberate. She can hurt me like this when she wants to. It is something she keeps hidden until needed, like a famous last name. I wonder how hard it is for her to resist doing, if it is a constant struggle. I suppose for this reason alone I am glad I don't hold the same power over her. But I feel that I do understand. I know that revenge only works for the living. And I think of how if it was me dying in the street I would have wanted someone next to me, someone to lie and tell me it would be okay, a familiar face to focus on instead of a wide open sky darkening at its edges.

The breeze that was blowing earlier has vanished and the inside of the car feels hot and crowded as if we've taken on passengers.

"I'm sorry," I say. "Let's forget it." And I want to. I want to forget the whole thing. I want to believe that we are not different from each other, that our ideas of love and forgiveness are the same. "I'm sorry," I tell her. The bay looks calm and I remember why we came here in the first place. "It's hot," I say. "Let's take a swim."

It has been a record hot summer and the water is as warm as the air. We hold hands and wade out in our underwear, skimming seaweed with our toes. Her bra and panties are beige, slightly darker than her flesh. She leans forward and stirs circles in the water with her fingers. A thin breeze skims the surface and I can feel the goose bumps as they rise up out of my skin. A couple years ago, on a dare, I swam all the way to a dock on the other side of the bay where some friends picked me up. It was nearly two miles across and everyone called me crazy, but I did it anyway, to prove them wrong, to show them that I could. I stare out over the water and wonder if I could still make it. I can see the marina at Perry's Landing, its sailboats draped in strings of bulbs.

The soft bottom gives beneath my feet and finally we are waist-deep. The lights and shadows of the city form another city on the water's surface. Buildings ripple on the waves. We stand in the middle of the image, the water breaking against our stomachs. Looking at her I remember that we have already picked names for our unborn children, chosen the house we will live in. And I know that it is silly and naïve. It is all a long way off, but we have made plans together.

"Float with me," she says. I allow my legs to come up beneath me until I am weightless and resting on my back, the water like a mattress underneath. She is lying next to me and between us our hands are joined. For a while we float. The dark sky looks close enough to touch. And then I am picturing her father, staring up at the springy underside of a prison bunk. And I think of my own dad, sitting in his office taking phone calls. I imagine her uncle Charlie dying alone, the asphalt softening below him, everything becoming unimportant so quickly. And I realize that in my entire life I've never even met anyone who's been robbed. I can feel her hand tighten in mine.

"Hold on to me," she says. We've floated further out. "Don't let go."

And so I squeeze her hand. I grip it hard until my own hand cramps and aches from the effort. And though she doesn't make a sound, I know that it must hurt her too.

Harvesters

WHEN MAY CAME, tiny fissures cleaving the steel-gray sky, Ty packed the duffle his father had left him long ago and drove west. Every year was the same. The Harvest began in Texas and it was there where he joined the others, running the combines day and night in staggered lines that left wide swaths in the open fields like fingers through sand. By June they had passed through Oklahoma and on into Kansas where the world seemed flatter still and the wheat moved atop the earth like the shimmer of heat over a fire. Across into Colorado and back through Nebraska following the grain, they slept and ate in trailers too small for comfort and worked till the great sky bruised at its edges, pinks and reds and violets Ty had seen nowhere else. They spoke of little besides the Harvest, and knew each other by their jobs. They traded day wages for rolls of quarters and washed their clothes in empty laundromats. If they drank they did so quickly and with a purpose in mind, filling the corner booths of taverns where they were nameless. With August came the Dakotas, where they moved up East River until they reached Redfield where Ty knew a woman. They worked two full days and half another before the rain they'd left in Tyndall caught up with them. When it did, Ty went to see her.

The flat house stood stark and chipped white at the edge of the town. Shutters that had been bright blue the year before hung faded. How many years had he been coming here? The raised porch, which had always sagged, was gone, replaced by a set of concrete stairs with a wrought iron railing. Ty wondered who'd done the work. In the kitchen window, a candle burned in a wine bottle. The rain had let up some, but the sky was still dark. In the distance, a caravan of semis moved slowly along 212, a gray smudge against the surrounding fields. A black walnut stood in a corner of the open yard, the tire swing that had once been there gone, though the frayed rope remained, twisting in the wind.

Ty knocked twice. A full minute passed before there was any sound, and then another before the door opened. The inside of the house was dark and, though it was four in the afternoon, the woman standing there wore a silk night robe cinched at the waist. He recognized it immediately and felt better. Her hair was matted and her face clear of makeup. Ty tried to reconcile her with his memory. The woman pinned her head to her shoulder as though to crack her neck.

"I guess summer's about over then," she said. She stepped back, and shut the door. Ty ran his hand over the railing. A small pool had settled between the front door and the concrete landing. Whoever had built the shuttering had missed on the rise. Ty was halfway to the road when he heard the door open. "You'll catch your death out there," the woman said.

The TV was on in the living room, a game show with the sound turned low. The rain picked up and made a steady racket on the asphalt shingles. Ty moved a blanket and sat on the edge of the sofa. The woman sat opposite him in a brown recliner. She pushed an ashtray aside and crossed her bare legs on the coffee table.

"You been to Jilly's?"

"Got in this morning," Ty said. The woman shook her head.

"If you think I believe that..." Her voice trailed off, and she stared through the window above his head. "It's always raining when you come." The creases at the corners of her eyes looked deeper and she rubbed at them with her fingertips as though she sensed him looking. "They cut my shifts down anyway." Ty remembered her moving behind the bar, fixing drinks and smiling. He remembered cupping her hand that first time, stopping her before she could turn to go.

The woman looked down from the window. "Where you headed next?" she asked.

"Let me take you to dinner," Ty said. She stared at him, her eyes hard-set and unblinking. Last year she'd told him to not come back. "Just pass right through," she'd said.

"Same as always," Ty said. "Up through Jamestown and Minot, maybe Montana if the weather holds and those others don't beat us to it."

"And if they do?"

Ty stood and ran his hands over the front of his jeans.

"Come on," he said. "Get ready. Anywhere you want."

They drove to Ashton, and stopped at the only restaurant there. Ty parked near the street and she was out with the door shut before he'd put the truck in park. They sat at a booth with a tiny jukebox on the table and water glasses so small he wondered if they were a joke. It was early still for dinner and the place was empty. She'd put her hair up and wore a yellow sundress with white trim he'd never seen before. She looked pretty, but he hadn't told her so. A young waitress in nurse's scrubs took their order.

"You want music?" he said, rifling through his pocket for leftover quarters.

"And ruin our conversation?" she asked. He laid his hands flat on the Formica tabletop and smiled. She lowered her head, but he thought he saw her do the same. Outside the rain was coming down in silvery sheets, filling the potholes in the gravel lot.

"Those stairs are nice," he said. "What happened to your porch?" Now she smiled full on, showing him again the way her front teeth on the bottom overlapped some. He'd forgotten.

"Never mind that," she said.

"It's a nice renovation."

"Yep," she said and nodded. "One of several."

They ate Swiss steak and homemade kuchen for dessert. Halfway through their meal, the rain stopped and there was a break in the sky. He stared at it, and when she saw, she stood to use the bathroom. He wondered if she was crying, but she returned quickly, and without even a streak in the powder she'd put on at home.

"It'll be pheasant season soon," he said. "Business will pick up. You might get yourself some of those shifts back."

"I've got other plans," she said. "And they don't center on ring-necks."

"What do they center on?"

"A whole lot of none-of-your-business." She was older now, but could still sound like a girl. She'd had plans before, and when the waitress stuck her head out from the kitchen to check on them, he lifted his empty coffee mug.

They took 281 toward Redfield. A small pocket of blue had opened above them and the sun sat at its center, curling back the clouds like a flame through plastic. He had belts to tighten on the draper header, teeth to replace on the reel, but it had rained for the better part of the day and he could see the stagnant pools in the fields all around them.

"It hasn't been like this everywhere," he said. "Colorado was so dry there was hardly a crop to work." She bent down and pumped the window crank until the cab filled with wind that carried the yeasty smell of the wet grain.

"Don't talk to me about the crop," she said.

A tan pickup was parked diagonally in her gravel drive. It was a dually with polished chrome exhaust stacks and white lettering on the side. When she saw that he had no intention of stopping she shook her head.

"No," she said, but Ty kept driving. He reached for her hand and she pulled it away.

"You think you're owed anything?" she asked him. "Even a day?"

"That's not it," he said. "I sold them on Redfield. They wanted us to head straight to Selby."

"You should have let them," she said. She squeezed her eyes shut and made fists on her thighs. "I wish you'd had gone there instead." She opened her eyes and looked disappointed to find him still in the truck. A group of motorcycles passed them heading the other way.

"It's been dry up north," he said. "We'll be finished early. I could come back through. We could go away like we did that one time." He remembered the cabin they'd rented near the Cheyenne River. One room with cedar paneling and a fireplace, a propane cook stove on a table in the corner. On their second night they'd stood near the woodpile and watched a mustang drink from a streambed.

"Take me home, Ty. Please." The fields on either side of

them rolled away from the highway toward distant crests. Ahead, the shoulder widened and connected to a dirt access road where he could turn around. He eased off the accelerator. A group of starlings made a black circle in the sky. Ty thought of the man who owned that truck, sitting in the living room where he had sat only a little while before.

"I was all set to leave Jilly's that day," he said.

"Ty. *Please*."

"But then I saw you behind that bar." A gust of wind blew through the open cab and caught her hair up around her face. "I'd been all over by then, Margaret. I'd never seen anything so beautiful." They rode past the turnaround in silence. He thought he heard her crying, but did not turn to check. The highway banked east. When he reached for her hand again she let him take it.

They found a small motel outside Bonilla, a low-built strip of rooms on the side of the highway. The parking lot was empty, but a red vacancy sign burned in the office window. An old man sat behind the desk watching baseball on a portable television. Ty got a room while she waited in the truck.

Inside he undressed her slowly. He touched those places on her body that had never grown familiar. The white curtains were yellowed by the sun and let in a half-light that illuminated the walls in sepia. He moved atop her carefully and when he finished he remained there, his face buried in her neck. Her hair smelled a mix of shampoo and smoke.

In the middle of the night, he woke suddenly, his heart beating a wild rhythm. He crawled off the thin mattress, careful not to wake her, and walked to the window. He drew back the curtain, and looked out over the darkened highway where no cars passed. In the morning he would service the combine and when the crop had dried, they would finish the final cut.

After the grain had been hauled away, they would load the combines onto the flatbeds while the farmer took a match to his fields to clear the stubble and weeds that remained. They would watch the rolling wave of fire as it crackled across the acres and filled the sky with smoke, and before it was out of sight, they would be gone.

A single chair sat in a corner and Ty placed it beside the bed and watched her sleep. The room was full dark, but his eyes had adjusted and he sat there, measuring her breaths against his own. She had been a young girl once, but she had never been his. He remembered again how he'd grabbed her hand so many years ago, and it seemed now like an awful thing to have done. From Redfield they would work their way through North Dakota and if Montana was spent they could head to Saskatchewan where there were farms that needed cut. Ty imagined them moving north forever, the vast horizon filled with a swaying grain unchanged over time. He imagined them working a Harvest that never ended, running their combines in steady lines that straddled the contours of the earth, filling their hoppers to overflowing, as time and again they reaped what they had not sown.

The Brother

ON SUNDAYS MAGGIE AND I never left my apartment. Sundays were for lying around, cooking Eggo waffles and bacon in our underwear, watching infomercials, having sex in the shower, and making promises we may not have made at any other time. This was our ritual, and we followed it the way other people went to church every week, or brunch. We were lying on the couch watching a woman on TV cut her son's hair with a vacuum cleaner. The light from outside was filtering in through my curtains and tiny particles of dust fell through the shafts of sunlight. Maggie was running her fingernails up and down the inside of my forearm when she said, "Would you hire Luke?"

Luke was Maggie's brother and had his own problems and so even in that relaxed state, without any hesitation, I said, "Luke is trouble."

"You used to be trouble," she said, pulling her hand away.

I had been with Maggie for almost a year and in that time had never told her much about my past. And I suppose because of that and for other reasons too, she had her suspicions.

"Not like that," I said, which was almost true. "I never knew trouble like that."

Luke was a few years younger than Maggie, and still lived at home with their parents in a studio apartment above the garage. He had just finished a four-month stretch in Erie County lock-up for appearing at a court date with half an ounce of schwag rolled tightly in a Ziploc bag he had neglected to remove from his coat pocket. Other than that, I didn't know much about him, just the little Maggie had told me and what I observed. He slept a lot, sometimes all day. He had mental health issues, at least that's what Maggie called them, for which he took prescriptions and sometimes saw a therapist, but more often than not he self-medicated. He'd been in a lot of car wrecks, usually with his being the only car involved, one time driving off the road and flipping upside down into a ditch. The few times I'd met him he seemed spaced-out and unresponsive, like only his body was there. He was tall and stringy, hardly filling the faded T-shirts and baggy jeans with frayed cuffs that served as his uniform. And he always stood hunched over, head down, like a child being reprimanded. A week earlier, he'd slipped into his parents' room as they slept and stolen his mother's jewelry off her nightstand. Two days later he reappeared, stumbling into the house in the middle of breakfast. Maggie's parents had given him an ultimatum, one last chance to get clean, or else they'd press charges and he'd go back to jail, which, with his record, would mean time at the state prison in Albion. They'd given him last chances before, but Maggie said this time they were serious.

Maggie flipped onto her side to face me. "Couldn't you just give him a shot?" she asked. "If it doesn't work out you can fire him." She was wearing a white tank top, revealing the tan, freckled skin of her chest. Maggie was a hostess at

Francine's, an upscale French restaurant down near Lake Erie, a job for which she was required to wear only black and to act disinterested. Maggie however was a naturally pleasant person and all of that snubbing took a toll on her. By the time she'd let herself into my apartment the night before, she was so exhausted from being rude that she'd neglected to wash off her makeup. Dark mascara caked her eyelashes, and a smudge of black cherry lipstick extended from the corner of her mouth. She looked beautiful in an unfinished way. "Besides, Sam," she said, "you could use the company."

I was a housepainter, a career I'd chosen when the time came for three reasons. College was an impossibility, I was not bothered by monotony, and most importantly, I wanted to work alone. It had been eight years, and I'd never even hired someone on part time. My days were spent on ladders, painting the sides of houses with fine even strokes. My nights were spent with Maggie. That was my life, uncomplicated by design.

"I don't know," I said. "What if things don't work out? Then I'm gonna be the guy who's sending your brother back to jail." My relationship with Maggie was good, and I didn't want anything getting in the way of that. She was content in our life, allowing me my silences when I needed them and otherwise staying close. She seemed happy where other women had not.

Maggie laid her hand on my naked chest and spread her fingers. "No, you'll be the guy who's keeping him out of jail right now," she said. "Just give him a chance. After that, it's on him."

The next morning I picked up Luke at his parents' house. He was standing at the end of their driveway with his head down, holding a brown paper bag. Except that he was finishing a cigarette he looked like a kid going off to his first day of school. I pulled up and he climbed into my truck. He put his lunch on the floor and strapped on his seat belt and halfway to the jobsite he said, "Thanks," while staring straight ahead, and that was it.

It was the beginning of summer and heat rose from the pavement in waves. We lived in Pennsylvania on the edge of Lake Erie, where for eight months out of the year the weather was shit, four months of freezing temperatures and snow sandwiched between two-month spans of rain. When the weather was like that I picked up whatever work I could, plowing driveways or hanging drywall, but when May arrived, the sun reappearing as though it had never left us, I painted houses.

For the first week, the only time I let Luke touch a brush was to clean it. Other than that his job was simple, spread the drop cloths along the perimeter of the house, unload the ladders and paint cans, and wait by the truck until it was time to leave. I figured the less that was expected of him, the less chance he had of fucking up. So he sat on the tailgate, and kicked up tiny dust storms, and smoked cigarettes until I was finished. Most days the sun outlasted us. I drank water from a disposable gallon jug, and stripped off my shirt when it became heavy with sweat, the sun turning my pale back the color of ripe cherries. At least I had the work to distract me from the heat, but Luke never complained of boredom or unfair treatment; he just sat and observed, and I took notice of that.

I could always tell if Luke was high when I arrived to pick him up. On mornings when he was, he filled the truck with an odor like burnt plastic. His skin was oilier, his acne more pronounced. It was as though every imperfection was magnified. His eyes, which were deeply set to begin with, seemed to have receded further back into his head, and when our gazes met, something he tried his best to avoid, it was as though he were looking out at me from behind a mask. But he was always waiting for me when I drove up, his head down, a cigarette pinched between his thumb and forefinger like a joint. He never missed a day and I never told Maggie he was using. His parents had forbidden him to leave the house except for work so I figured whatever he was on was a holdover stash and that he'd run out before long. And besides, I wasn't a narc. There were times when I even felt a sort of kinship with him. We had both grown up in the same place, had both used Erie's meager size and limited diversions as an excuse to drink our parents' liquor, steal beer from their garages, raid their medicine cabinets. I knew that when he'd started in on that kind of life his intention had not been to waste his days. I knew because that had not been my intention either. It was just the opposite, like you were living more fully than everyone else. I knew what it was like to look at the people around you and mistake their fear for envy, their pity for admiration. I knew also what it was like to wake up in a hospital room, one arm connected to an IV, the other handcuffed to the bedrail, your best friend dead in a car you were driving. I knew what it was like to have a policeman look at you like you were the lowest thing on earth and tell you the wreck was so twisted that emergency crews had to cut the legs off the corpse to remove it. I knew what it was like to finally realize the things you had done and beg a young doctor to kill you with morphine.

Eventually I began to let Luke do some actual work. I started him off slowly, painting sheds and garages with a roller before moving him to a straight-edge siding brush and having him work on the houses with me. He was a quick learner, attentive and cautious until he felt he had a certain technique down, and by the Fourth of July I had taught him almost everything I could about primer and feathering and following the sun around a house. At first, when I'd round the corner of some old Victorian and find him working on the next side, it surprised me, as though we were meeting by chance encounter, but gradually I came to depend on him being there, using a hook scraper to remove old paint, or masking the windows with heavy plastic. He worked slowly but he was more than competent, and sometimes we finished in a day what would have taken me two. Maggie had the Fourth off work and wanted to go watch the fireworks display at Mercyhurst College. She had told me to invite Luke. She said he was probably starving for some social interaction since their parents had him on lock down, so on the way home from work I mentioned it.

"I don't know," he said, staring at his hands. "I'm kind of on house arrest."

"Maggie cleared it with your folks," I said, feeling bad. Luke was in his early twenties and basically grounded. His parents wouldn't even let me pay him. We were driving along East Lake Road past a line of row houses, squat and dark, and then Hammermill, an abandoned paper plant that had closed when I was a kid. It was a huge red brick building with busted out windows and an overgrown jungle of a parking lot. As teenagers we would hop the fence and break in. Even then, years after the giant metal presses had stopped stamping out sheets, the place still reeked of the sulfur used to cook the wood chips. We had started bonfires on the cold concrete floors with reams of old paper, our shadows dancing along the gray water-stained walls.

I nodded toward the ancient brick structure. "Kids used to break in there to get fucked up," I said.

Luke followed my gaze, his face filling with something like nostalgia. "They still do," he said. He continued staring out my window long after Hammermill had fallen behind us, as though he were in a trance. "Alright then," he finally said. "I'll go."

Mercyhurst was close to my apartment so the three of us walked over together. I lived in a decent neighborhood, the kind of street where you were more likely to have your car side-swiped than your place broken into. I had taken the apartment near the college because the rent was cheap. On weekend nights during the school year, I could hear drunk college students walking to off-campus parties, laughing and yelling, shattering bottles, singing loudly. But it was summer and most of the students had gone home. Instead, the sidewalks were crowded with packs of kids carrying sparklers in each hand, their faces lit in blues and reds like tiny apparitions.

The college set off their show from the football stadium. No one was allowed into the staging area, but there was a wide field out back where you could watch. By the time we arrived the grass was already covered. We found a spot near the back of the field, close to a chain link fence, and spread the blanket Maggie had brought.

"So, Luke," Maggie said, "how do you like working with Sam?"

Luke shifted uncomfortably near the edge of the blanket.

"I like it," he said.

"Well you must be doing a good job. You're the only person Sam ever let work with him." Luke looked over at me as though to test the validity of this statement and I nodded. I had seen Maggie flatter him for little things, like being on time, or combing his hair. She was trying to boost his self-esteem, and draw him out, but the praise was so over-the-top that I wondered if it made him uneasy.

I leaned back on my elbows. Behind the chain link fence was a basketball court. A couple of kids were goofing around, running at the backboard and leaping in the air, trying to grab the rim.

Maggie said, “Did you know that Luke was quite a basketball player in his day?”

“He never mentioned,” I said.

“He was the best on his team, all the way through junior high.”

Luke was sitting in front of us hugging his knees to his chest. He rocked slightly from side to side. Maggie leaned in close and put her lips next to my ear. “He was a good student, too,” she whispered, “before he started getting in trouble. My parents want him to take a few classes this fall.”

I heard a noise like a giant bottle rocket and watched as the first firework shot into the air, its tail slashing a white tear through the dark sky. It reached its pinnacle and hung there before exploding in a giant burst of sparks that fell like the leaves of a weeping willow. The explosion echoed across the field and Maggie squeezed my arm where I hadn't even noticed she was holding it. On the blanket in front of us, a little boy jumped into his mother's arms, and somewhere a baby began to cry. Behind us two groups of boys had congregated at opposite sides of the basketball court and were firing Roman Candles at each other, screaming wildly as they dodged tiny balls of fire in an eerily miniaturized imitation of war. I looked at Luke, hoping to gauge his reaction to the fireworks, and found him trying to light a cigarette, shielding a match from the breeze with a cupped hand.

We left before the show ended, the three of us walking slowly through the smoky night. Along the road that led back to my neighborhood were some of the buildings that made up the college, low brick structures with glass entrances that glowed like blank television screens. I tried to imagine Luke walking in and out of those buildings, a book bag strapped to his back. I tried to envision him talking to girls in the quad, or throwing a football with his friends, or sitting in a classroom, taking notes as he listened to his professors tell him how the world was supposed to work. But it was hard to picture him there, not just because of what I knew about him, but because of all I didn't know about places like that. And for some reason, that made me want it for him even more.

A week later I got the kind of job that could set me up for the whole year, one that would pay my bills with enough left over to take Maggie for a weekend at one of the fancy B&Bs that sat along the lake in Northeast. The place was a mansion on South Shore Drive, the area of town where all of Erie's real money lived; the owner, a widow, told me over the phone that her husband would have wanted her to keep the place looking good. South Shore Drive was a half-mile long stretch of mansions set on a cliff above Presque Isle Bay. A couple hundred feet below was the Erie Yacht Club with its cream-colored lighthouse and rows of slips occupied by six-figure sailboats. Most of the homeowners were old people who rarely went out, so the traffic was mainly comprised of the landscapers who spent their days planting annuals and trimming hedges. The rest of the traffic was made up of people driving to Sunset Point, a narrowly paved pull off at the end of the street. People drove there to watch the sun bleed its colors across the sky before falling into the lake. The day after the woman answered my ad in the yellow pages, Luke and I drove over for a walk around.

The place was huge, a two-story off-white structure with Roman columns and a fountain in the center of the yard. A concrete path led to the front door, and as we approached, we saw that the columns were crumbling near the base, some shingles hung loosely from the edge of the roof, and several of the window sashes were rotted. Before I could knock, the door opened to reveal a tall, sturdy woman, probably in her seventies, wearing black trousers and a matching sweater set. She wore a silver crucifix and had the elegant, neatly managed hairstyle of a politician's wife. She reached out to shake my hand before I had the chance to offer it.

"Thank you for coming on such short notice," she said. "I'm Mrs. Curtze, but please call me Peggy." She moved past me and shook Luke's hand.

"Nice to meet you, ma'am," he said.

"Please, call me Peggy."

Luke hesitated and then said, "Nice to meet you, Peggy." For a couple of weeks Luke had been straight when I'd arrived to pick him up. His eyes had begun to take on a lucid quality, as though everything that had clouded them was finally being flushed from his system. He worked faster and our trips to and from jobs were no longer silent, but filled with small talk, the kind of loose chatter I suspected people in office buildings exchanged during coffee breaks. The only negative side effect of his sobriety was his smoking. When I'd first hired him he went through a pack a day, but now, if he bought a carton of Camel Wides on Monday it was gone by Thursday, and more than once I'd had to make an emergency stop in between jobsites. The tips of his fingers turned as yellow as scorched grass and he kept an empty Dutch Boy can near wherever he was working to use as an ashtray.

"Would either of you like something to eat or drink?" Peggy asked.

"No thank you. We just finished breakfast," I said, which wasn't true. We'd stopped at a Country Fair gas station on our way over where all I'd bought was coffee while Luke waited in the truck and smoked. But something about Peggy, maybe the fact that she was rich or old or both, made me think she'd look down upon two men skipping breakfast, and I didn't want that. I wanted her to like us.

Peggy led us around the house, pointing out where time and weather had done their work, showing us where the paint had begun to peel away in short curls like pencil shavings. The back of the house faced the bay and was in the worst shape of all. Most of the trim was gone and entire strips of siding had been exposed. Luke pulled a piece of paint from the corner of the house and examined it.

"It's lead-based," he said.

"Is that bad?" Peggy asked.

"It's toxic," Luke said. "They don't even use it anymore."

"Oh my," Peggy said, as though Luke were a doctor who'd just diagnosed her with some fatal disease. "Will you be able to remove it?"

"It's not a big deal," I said. "We'll just have to be careful stripping it. Do you know when the house was built?"

"We bought it in '87, but I'm not sure when it was built. The early sixties maybe? My husband was the one who kept track of all that." She smiled at me sheepishly as though embarrassed that she couldn't answer my question. "Albert passed away last year."

"Sorry to hear that," I said.

Luke dropped the piece of paint, and watched as the wind sent it skittering along the short grass. Near the edge of the lawn was a wooden deck with a staircase at one end that disappeared over the side of the cliff. "Have you found any dead animals around the outside of your house lately?" Luke asked.

Peggy looked shocked. "No, I mean, not that I know of, but the gardener takes care of everything outdoors."

"'Cause lead paint can kill them," he said. "Children too, if they get into it."

Peggy's face took on a look of genuine concern. "Oh my goodness," she said.

"It's toxic," Luke said again. "You'd be responsible if someone was hurt." His words were clipped and sharp. He sounded like a parent reprimanding their child.

I shot Luke a look and he stopped talking. "It's not likely the paint chips harmed anything, although it's a good idea to repaint."

Peggy looked at the back of the house, letting her eyes wander up and down as though she were seeing the damage for the first time. "I'm learning a lot of new things lately," she said, "things I didn't have to worry about before." A robin shot across the sky in a red flash and disappeared past the tree-lined cliff. I tried to think of something to say but couldn't.

"Well thank you again for coming over so soon. I suppose time is of the essence in a situation like this," Peggy said, turning toward me.

"It's really not that big a deal," I said. "It'll be just fine."

We walked to the truck where I gave her some color samples and thanked her for calling. Then Luke and I got in and drove off. I waited until we'd turned off South Shore before talking.

"What the hell was that all about?"

"What do you mean?" Luke asked, cranking down his window.

"Where'd you get all that shit about lead paint?"

"I read it on the Internet."

"Yeah, well you were being a real hard-on. I wouldn't blame her if she called to tell me she'd found someone else to paint her house."

"Who cares?" Luke said. He lit a cigarette and slipped his lighter back into his pocket. "All that money and she can't even keep her house from falling apart. She doesn't even know when it was built."

"What's that to you?" I said. "Besides, I really need that job and you almost blew it for us."

"*Us*?" Luke said. He was staring out the window, but I could see his face in the side view. His eyes were narrow and angry. "You don't even pay me," he said without turning around.

"That wasn't my decision, Luke," I said, "and it's not something I feel good about either." A red SUV cut into the lane in front of me and I slowed down.

Luke let out a quick laugh. "I bet you're real torn up about it," he said.

"Think what you want, Luke, but you brought that on yourself. You brought all of this on yourself."

Luke flicked his cigarette out the window.

"What would you know about it?" he said. And he said it in a way that made me think he might actually have wanted me to answer. Outside, Erie's lower west side flashed by in a gray blur, plastics factories and bars and tool and die shops. I hit some potholes and the steel extension ladders rattled against the roof. I thought about pulling over, stopping, and telling him the things I knew that I was sure he didn't. But even my thoughts sounded wrong, like complaints, so I leaned forward and switched on the radio, turning up the volume until I couldn't even hear myself breathe.

That night I picked up Maggie at Francine's. She had split her shift with another hostess and when I arrived she was waiting on a bench across the street from the restaurant. It was still light out and Maggie was smiling, a plastic to-go bag cradled in her lap. I reached across the truck's interior and swung open the passenger door.

"You going my way?" she asked in her pretend sexy voice, a throaty vibrato that always ended with her giggling.

"I am now," I said, taking the bag from her as she climbed in.

On nights when Maggie got off work early we would drive out to Presque Isle, the sandy peninsula half a mile wide that curved into Lake Erie like a dog's tail. The entrance gate was closed when it got dark, but once you were in you could leave when you wanted. We didn't go for the beach or the sand or for the murky water of the lake. Nobody did. We went for the sunsets, intense explosions that ignited the clouds. For those few minutes every day it looked like the lake was on fire, a giant all-consuming blaze far out on the horizon. Erie's sunsets were world-class. Something about the pollution.

Maggie and I sat down at a picnic table. She put the bag on the carved-up surface and took out a loaf of crusty bread and two aluminum foil containers folded to look like swans. She opened them, and a tiny cloud of steam rose into the cool air.

"Steak au Poivre," she said, handing me a set of plastic utensils.

"Sounds good."

Down the beach two men sat on a blanket holding hands, watching the sun disappear into the lake.

"How was the new job?" Maggie asked.

"Not bad," I said. "A nice lady. A widow. She's got a big place over on South Shore. It's gonna take us a while."

Maggie slid closer to me on the bench. "How's Luke doing?"

She asked me about Luke every day. It was the first thing she brought up when she saw me, and she always wanted to know all the details: what we talked about, how his mood seemed, what he'd had for lunch.

"Fine," I said.

"Fine?" she repeated. "How do you mean fine?"

"I don't know, just fine," I said, more harshly than I intended. I took a bite of the tender, peppery steak. Maggie was looking out where the sun had gone down. A smoky violet haze sat on the water. At the end of the beach, the two men stood, folded their blanket, and walked toward the parking lot. Maggie and I were alone. The food was getting cold, and I wasn't hungry anyway. I closed the foil over the steak. Maggie was still staring out, like she was waiting for something to appear. I put my hand on the small of her back.

"We should go," I said. "It's late."

Without turning toward me Maggie said, "You can't hide this from me, you know." Her voice was soft but definite.

"I wouldn't."

"Yes, you would," she said sharply. "It's what you do." A breeze worked its way across the water and up the beach, rustling the plastic bag. Tiny waves rolled against the stone breakers offshore. I thought about all the nights Maggie and I had spent together, how it reassured me to know she was there, that all I had to do was reach over to feel the warmth of her skin. I thought about how many times I had woken in the darkest hours of the night, cold with sweat, all my demons waiting on the other side of sleep. It was then that I wanted most to tell her everything, afraid of how it might sound, afraid of having to go back there. I stopped myself every time, reaching for her instead.

The edge of the picnic table was splintered. I ran my fingers along it. "You were the one who wanted me to hire Luke," I said.

"That's not the point."

"Then what is?" I asked. I was trying to keep my voice steady, but there was anger in it. Maggie stared at me for what felt like a long time, studying my face until I had to look away.

"Listen to me," she said. "You don't have to tell me why you never drink, or why sometimes you won't talk for days, or how you got that scar on your back, but not *this*. That other stuff...it's yours, but not this. Luke is my brother, and I need to know. Do you understand?" Her eyes were trained on me as she waited for her answer. After a moment, I nodded and she stood up. She lifted the leftovers from the table and walked off and scattered them for the gulls. She stood, staring out at the water like at any moment she might step in. After a while she turned around, and when she came back we left.

The next day over tuna salad sandwiches Luke apologized to me. We were sitting in my truck with the air conditioner running, eating lunch while our sweat-soaked shirts cooled and dried. We'd spent the whole morning wet-scraping the paint, double bagging the peels into heavy duty garbage bags that were piled high in the bed of the truck. I had sensed that the apology was coming, and I dreaded it.

"I don't know why I acted that way," Luke said. "I know you're doing me a favor here."

"Just forget about it," I said. "It's in the past. It never happened."

"Are you sure? 'Cause I feel real bad about all the shit I said. It's just that sometimes..." Luke paused. He stared at the dash, concentrating to find words. "It's like I lose myself sometimes, like I change into someone else." He looked embarrassed. "Does that make any sense?" he asked.

I thought that it did, that sometimes we were not the people whom we claimed to be or who others thought us to be, but different entirely, as though possessed. And because of it we could never fully know anyone, and trying too hard to figure it out would always be a losing game. I palmed the sweat from my face.

"Luke," I said, "all that stuff yesterday, it's water under the bridge. Alright?" I took a drink of Coke and pressed the cold can against my forehead before returning it to the cup holder.

"Alright then," Luke said, his voice quiet. "Alright."

After that things seemed to return to pretty much the way they had been. I picked up Luke in the mornings and on the way over to South Shore Drive we'd stop at Country Fair. I still bought my coffee and Luke still bought his cigarettes, but I'd get us a couple of sausage and egg biscuits too, just in case Peggy asked. We worked steadily, scraping the house and garage, making regular trips to the hazardous waste site across town to drop off the bags of old paint. After we'd finished with the stripping, we sanded the wood and painted on a clear water-repellant. By the end of July we'd finished applying the primer and Peggy chose a shade of taupe, which for some reason made me like her even more. We bought every can they had in stock at Value Home Center. But August started off wet. For a week straight it did nothing but storm. I picked up Luke anyways, mostly because Maggie said it wouldn't be good for him to sit around the house all day, and I had nothing to do either. We had coffee at Panos Diner and stared out the front windows beyond the lunch counter, watching the gray sky and the rain as it hit the street and drew the oil up out of the asphalt. Every once in a while the weather would break, but usually not till late afternoon when it was too late to start working anyway. I'd pay our check and we'd just drive around aimlessly for a while, making turns for no other reason than how the road was banked. We drove without talking, past the city limits, out toward Fairview or Waterford where the pavement gleamed, slick with rain. We stopped at roadside stands for sweet corn and the last of that year's strawberries, wine-colored and over ripe, which we ate until our mouths looked bloodied.

Finally the storms passed, blown inland by the lake. We returned to Peggy's and applied the finish coats, spacing them two weeks apart and beginning a few smaller projects in the meantime. A week after we'd finished the trim and packed up our brushes and ladders and drop cloths, after we'd walked Peggy around the house to make sure she approved of our work, which she did, flattering us all the while, I drove over to thank her one last time for hiring us and to leave her the invoice. I rang the doorbell and waited for what seemed like a long time. It was Saturday and I'd called before I'd left to make sure she'd be home. She sounded genuinely happy when I asked if I could stop by and had told me to come right over. I rang the bell again and waited awhile longer. I was beginning to worry that maybe Peggy had fallen. I checked the door. It was unlocked and so I pushed it open, stepped inside, and called her name. The foyer was large and white with a wide staircase that rose to a landing and then on to the upstairs hall. A round skylight filled the room with filtered sunlight, and left a bright circle on the marble floor. Opposite the staircase was a long rectangular glass-topped table in the center of which stood an arrangement of fake lilies in a vase. I held the invoice and thought briefly about just leaving it there, but I had become nervous at Peggy's not answering. An image of her, collapsed on the floor, popped into my mind. I had never been in the house and felt slightly uneasy as I passed through the front hall.

"Anybody home?" I called out. "Peggy?" The hall was dimly lit and smelled like old fruit. Framed pictures hung on the wall: family portraits, a painting of the peninsula, an old grainy black and white picture of a young Peggy standing on a beach somewhere. In the picture Peggy was wearing one of the modest swimsuits of the day and smiling, head cocked to one side knowingly. "Peggy?" I said continuing down the hall, "You home?" I stepped into what must have been the great room and saw Peggy sitting on a couch near a wide granite fireplace, her head bent down and her lips moving slowly, soundlessly, as though reading to herself. Her white hair was flattened on one side like she'd been lying down, and her eyes were squeezed shut. A man sat beside her watching me.

"Hello," he said calmly. He was wearing a black t-shirt and jean shorts, and he had on high work boots with the laces tied around them. He smiled and squinted. "Talk about bad timing, huh?" he said. With his left hand he held a screwdriver to the fleshy underside of Peggy's neck. The handle had been wrapped in what looked like black electrical tape.

"She's praying," the man said. Then, as though he'd just remembered what he was doing there, he said, "My partner is upstairs. He has a gun so don't try anything or I'll yell." He said this in a hurried way, like the moderator of some meeting rushing through formalities. I stood stock-still. My arms felt heavy, and dangled awkwardly beside me. I was holding the invoice and thought of putting it in my pocket, but realized it wouldn't be a good idea.

"Do you read lips?" the man asked. I heard footsteps above me and then something large and solid hitting the floor. The man looked at me impatiently.

"No. I'm sorry."

He let out a long disappointed breath, like a teenager exhaling cigarette smoke for effect. "Don't be. Who reads lips? I just can't make out what she's saying." The man stared intently at Peggy's mouth. "I only know she's praying because

I can tell when she says God." He pulled the screwdriver away from her neck and rubbed his temple with the handle before returning it. "There," he said suddenly, "she just said it. Come here. See if you can figure out the rest." He waved me over.

I walked slowly, my hands out to either side like I'd seen in the movies, and sat down in an overstuffed leather chair that faced the couch.

"Now pay attention," he said. "I might quiz you on this later." He looked at me and smiled. His eyes were red-rimmed and he had a sparse line of black hair above his top lip like a teenager's first mustache. His hair was black and combed straight back.

I moved toward the edge of the chair. "Peggy," I said, "it's Sam."

"*Don't*," the man said, turning toward me. He pointed the screwdriver at me in an accusatory way, his index finger extending over the dull metal. "Don't you fucking do that. Let her pray." The outburst was sudden and furious.

"I'm sorry." I inched back in the seat. Adjacent to where we sat was a large window, revealing the wide expanse of the back yard and the bay beyond it. The day had been windy and the water was choppy with whitecaps. Clouds were gathering over the lake, and the sky was gray and ashy. I heard footsteps and turned around and saw another man standing near where I'd come in. He was tall with a shaved head and loose-fitting jeans that hung from his hips. He had on a green flannel shirt and a backpack.

"You make a new friend?" he asked the other man.

The man beside Peggy laughed. "Yes, I guess I did."

"I'm doing all the work and you're entertaining," the other man said, and he did not say it in a kind way. "Are you alone?" he asked me.

I nodded.

"Good," he said. He took off his backpack and set it on the ground before unzipping it. He fumbled around inside, searching for something. After a moment he pulled out a gun and pointed it at me. "See," he said. "I guess I won't have to show you again, will I?"

"No."

"Alright then," he said. He put the gun back in the bag and zipped it up before slinging it onto his back. "Alright," he said again, and walked over to us.

"Did you get everything?" the man beside Peggy asked.

"Wasn't a whole lot to get. Isn't that right, you?" the man said raising his voice in Peggy's direction, but Peggy kept her head down and continued to pray. The man reached toward her and for a moment I thought he might hit her. My body tightened in anticipation, and helplessness consumed me. But the man simply plucked off Peggy's earrings like someone removing ornaments from a Christmas tree. He dropped them in his pocket and turned to me.

"And what about you?" the man said. "I wouldn't want to forget about you."

I dug my wallet out of my back pocket and handed it to him and he gave it to his partner.

"Watch?" he said, and I held up my naked wrist and he nodded in a satisfied way.

"And what's that?" he said, pointing at the invoice.

"It's nothing," I said, "just a bill for some work I did."

The man looked at me as though I were joking and then began to laugh.

"She might be a while paying you," he said still laughing, and then he took the invoice from my hand and read it. "Holy shit, that's some bill. What'd you do, fuck her?"

The man sitting beside Peggy let out a sharp laugh. "What's he charging her?"

"Too much," the other man said. He was standing over me looking down. He smelled like stale cigarettes and he shook his head, disappointed. He read the heading on the invoice out loud. "Sam's House Painting Service," he said, and then smiled to himself. He was trying to make up his mind about something. When he spoke again it was as though he were surrendering to some beautiful impulse. "Well, shit," he said, "you're worse than us, charging this much with free labor." He crumpled up the paper and dropped it. "Come on," he said to the other man. "Time to go."

They walked out of the room in the direction of the backyard, and in a moment I saw them through the window, crossing the wide lawn in a way that was not at all hurried. I wondered if Luke was waiting for them in a car somewhere, ready to disappear. I could already feel him vanishing. I knew that Maggie would blame me, and that in time she would vanish too, emptying her things from my apartment, clearing herself from my life.

I got up and walked to the window and when the two men had nearly reached the deck the one with the backpack stopped and turned around. The other man hesitated for a moment but continued on disappearing down the stairs. The one who remained stood staring at the back of the house, scanning it from the top down until finally he saw me standing there in the window. I had my hand up, pressed against the glass and our eyes met and he smiled and said something I could not decipher and then he held up his own hand in the same fashion as mine, palm out fingers extended, the way you might wave to someone you didn't really know, or how people in the movies said goodbye to someone in prison, someone buried behind a wall of glass who had done something wrong and was paying for it, someone who no matter how hard you tried you would never touch again.

Hunters

THE WINTER I TURNED twenty-seven, I followed a woman who said she might love me to a small town in Northwest Pennsylvania, a go-between place that provided me with little comfort, except maybe to say that its prospects seemed even worse than my own. By the time the woman I'd followed left me, clearing out our meager apartment while I was at work, I had already established a routine. Mornings and afternoons I worked cooking wood chips into a mealy pulp at the paper mill near the lake. Evenings I went to Hunters Tavern, the place where I did most of my drinking.

Hunters was a small, dark bar, close enough to where I was staying that I could walk. The prices were good and the same ten or fifteen men were always sitting at the bar when I arrived, quiet men who would not bother you, but who you could have a friendly conversation with if the topic and the timing were right. At the far end of the bar, encased in glass, was a large black bear the previous owner had killed and had professionally mounted. A small fake tree stood on one side of the case and a landscape painting covered the back wall. It displayed a grass-filled valley with a thin stream running through it and tall mountains in the distance. The bear had been fixed in an attack pose, claws extending from outstretched paws, jaws opened wide revealing a row of sharp, yellowed teeth. A single light bulb at the top of the display illuminated the whole thing, casting the bear's dark shadow across the hardwood.

There were rarely any women at Hunters, except for the wives of a few of the regulars, who would come to pick up their husbands at closing. These were women who stood in the doorway silently, hair mussed from sleep, long winter coats held shut over fraying nightgowns. Their faces were aged with the stoic acceptance of their lots, and they would wait until their husbands finished the drinks they had in front of them, unseated themselves clumsily from their stools, and collected their change and cigarettes from the bar.

On most nights I would sit at the end of the bar by myself, watching whatever game might be playing on the television mounted in the corner or staring at the bear behind the glass. But on this night, the one I'm going to tell you about, I was shooting pool with a man who came to Hunters twice daily for his meals, which he took alone in a corner booth. The bar had only one pool table, an off-balance affair with loose felt, torn in spots and covered with cigarette burns. The house cues were all a bit warped and so there were several variables to even the most straightforward shots. We weren't playing for anything, just killing time while he waited for his dinner. It was the end of January and outside a freezing rain coated the streets in ice, so the bar had been mostly empty all night. It was late and I was thinking of leaving when the glass door swung open and a woman came in alone. She wasn't wearing a coat and once the door had shut behind her, she shook her entire body the way a dog might while trying to dry itself off. Tiny pieces of ice had settled in her long brown hair and even in the dim light of the bar they sparkled. She stood for a moment by the doorway and let her eyes wander around the room as though she might be searching for someone in particular. Her gaze passed right over me and everyone else and when she'd finished she turned and moved toward the bar. She was wearing boots with heels on them and stumbled slightly as she walked.

The man I was playing pool with looked at the woman and then at me and shook his head and smirked. He sank the eight ball with a decent cut and then took a seat in his booth to wait for his chicken wings. I walked back over to the end of the bar and ordered another drink. The woman was sitting a few stools down, stirring a glass of whiskey and ice with her pinky finger. There was nobody between us. I was trying to see her face but her hair was blocking her profile. After a moment she pushed it aside and looked around and seemed to catch a glimpse of the bear. She got up and walked over and stood next to me.

"That's some animal," she said. "What do you suppose he was thinking the moment he got shot?"

"Probably, '*oh shit,*'" I said, without turning around. She laughed and so I invited her to sit down and she did.

"Doesn't seem right," she said, "a strong creature like that, locked away in here forever, to be stared at by drunks."

"Doesn't matter how it seems," I said, and for a moment I thought I'd said the wrong thing, that she would stand and walk away without another word, but instead she nodded.

"You're right," she said, "it doesn't." She looked at me and I saw traces of aged beauty, sharp features now covered with too much makeup, powder caked in places, mascara running a little from the rain. She was drunk, but not so much that she slurred her words, just enough so that I knew. On her left ring finger was a gold wedding band.

"Where's he tonight?" I asked, pointing at the ring.

"Burying his mother in Pittsburgh," she said.

"Why aren't you there?"

"Because I always hated his mother." She smiled, her tongue flicking against the back of her teeth and when the bartender came by again, I ordered us a round of shots.

It didn't take long, the two of us drinking the way we were. Soon I was driving her car along 26th Street, past the highway connector and a dark stretch of abandoned warehouses and factories. She'd told me she'd let me know when we reached her street, but it seemed like I'd been driving forever. She rolled her shoulders back and forth across the cloth seat as though, even sitting down, she was slightly off balance. Her eyes were squeezed shut, and she kept running her hand up and down my leg.

"Are we there yet?" she asked.

"You tell me."

She opened her eyes. "Next one," she said.

I turned off at the next street and drove slowly as I followed her directions. A thin layer of ice had formed on the asphalt and glinted under the streetlights. Finally I pulled into a narrow gravel driveway. Her house looked like every other house on the block. A small, two-story building with aluminum siding and a roof in disrepair. I shut off the headlights and the engine.

"This is it," she said. "*Tada*." And then she leaned across the middle console and kissed me hard, pushing against my lips until she'd pinned my head against the driver's side window. She tasted like some overripe fruit, spoiled and pungent, and she ran her tongue around the inside of my mouth. I thought about the woman I'd moved to that town for, where she might be at that very moment, who she might be there with.

The woman leaned back and took a deep breath. In front of us, the large bay windows of the house were illuminated by the amber glow of a streetlight. I saw that the curtains had been pulled back slightly and that there was a small girl inside, standing there watching us.

"Who's that?" I asked, nodding toward the window. The girl couldn't have been any older than six or seven. She had long blonde hair and wore a large white t-shirt that fell below her knees. Her tiny hand was pressed against the window and she looked scared. When she saw that we'd spotted her, she hid quickly behind the curtain.

The woman had followed my stare. "That's my daughter," she said. "She's supposed to be in bed."

"Who's watching her?"

The woman turned and gave me an annoyed look. "She's *supposed* to be in bed," she said again. "She watches herself."

All of this happened a long time ago. I no longer live in that town, or anywhere near it. And I no longer drink the way I once did, angry and hungry at the same time. These days I have a family of my own, a wife and a daughter who thinks I'm the world. At night, after I've tucked my daughter into bed, I wait outside her room for a minute, so that if she calls for me, I will hear. Every day I go to my job and come straight home after, and there are many, my family included, who would call me a good man. And it is maybe because of these things that it is hard for me to imagine *that* man, the one who got out of the car that night and stood quietly in the doorway while that woman screamed at her daughter, the girl shivering as cold air rushed in around me, pulling the hem of her makeshift nightgown toward the floor, the woman screaming and screaming until she finally sent the girl off to bed crying. I try to think of how that girl might have seen me, an uncertain creature silhouetted in the doorway, a strange man in her home, and it reminds me of the stains I've left on this life of mine. It's hard to think of that man, the one who stayed the night with that woman and left the next morning without a word. It is hard for me to picture him, but that does not change anything. And it is not regret I am talking about, it is something different altogether. I remember that when that woman yelled at her daughter she called her Lexie. The girl's name was Lexie.

This Too

MARTHA SCRUBS THE WINDOWS with a mixture of hot water and ammonia. She wonders when Benjy painted them black. It is night, but still, the effect is palpable. Outside, there's a half moon and streetlights casting their orange glow. Little gets through. Martha dips the sponge into the steaming bucket at her feet. She is not wearing gloves. The phone rings and she remembers she needs to call and cancel service. When the machine picks up there is silence and then a long beep. Whoever is on the other line waits a moment and then hangs up. Martha works until her hands are shriveled and pink. They remind her of the pet hamster she had as a child. When it gave birth to a litter she was so excited she picked one up to show her parents. That night the mother hamster ate the baby Martha had contaminated with her scent. When Benjy found out, he filled the bathroom sink and drowned the other babies one by one. Martha remembers him sitting on the edge of the tub. She remembers crying when she saw the hairless babies floating in the sink like severed thumbs. Benjy was calmer than she'd ever seen him. She remembers what he said as he brushed past her. *I saved them.* When Martha finally recovered herself, she flushed the babies and told her parents the mother had eaten them all.

Martha kneels and dips her arm up to the elbow in the hot water and ammonia. Tears fill her eyes. The pain creeps toward her shoulder. When she thinks she might pass out, she stands, shuts off the light and leaves.

On the drive home Martha thinks about the last time Benjy called, a month ago. His apartment is in Homestead, only a mile and a half from the house she shares with two roommates, but at the time she had no idea. She hadn't seen or heard from him in over a year. No one had. It was late, and she'd fumbled with the cell. When no one spoke on the other end, she knew it was him. *Where are you,* she whispered. For the longest time there was nothing. *I'm hiding,* he finally said, and hung up.

The next day Martha returns to the apartment. As she's turning the lock she sees a pair of eyes watching her from behind a cracked door down the hall.

Inside, she walks past the bathroom she refuses to enter. It is the one room she will not go into. In the bedroom, she sorts through Benjy's CDs and then his books. She lifts one off the floor and flips through its pages. Desperate scrawls in the margins, whole chapters blacked out in permanent marker. When the cops arrived, the walls were covered in writing. The landlord painted over it before Martha could see and she's grateful for that, but she knows whatever he wrote is still there, just hidden. He did the same thing when they were kids growing up in the suburbs of Pittsburgh. Locked in his room for two and a half days arguing loudly with himself. Martha remembers wishing he would let her in, so she could take care of him. When their father finally kicked down the door the walls were covered, diagrams and drawings and the same word written over and over.

Martha folds his clothes and stacks them into plastic trash bags, his jeans and t-shirts, his sweaters and hoodies, all of them threadbare and dark. She is tying the bags shut when she hears the knock. She walks down the hall, opens the door, and sees the eyes again, only now they belong to a body. A pale girl with wispy blonde hair and a tattoo of a rosary on her breastplate.

Are you the sister, she asks. Martha doesn't say anything, just stands there, staring through this girl who must have seen Benjy a thousand times since the last time she did. She digs her fingernails into the flesh of her palms. *I called last night,* the girl says.

Why would you do that?

I don't know. And now she is crying, her bottom lip quivering like there's a charge running through it. *He talked about you sometimes. I've never met anyone so scared.*

Inside, Martha and the girl sit on the carpet and stare at the walls. They look sweaty and slick from the new paint job, as though they are oozing. They are eggshell-white, a blank canvas for future tenants to hang their posters and pictures on. The girl is picking at the nap of the carpet, her nails bitten to the quick. Martha wants to ask this girl some questions, but knows the answers won't matter. Instead she tells her about the summer Benjy dreamed of being a smokejumper, how he walked around in a bicycle helmet, his parachute a backpack stuffed with an old bed sheet. *He always made me be the pilot.* Martha remembers how much she hated the game, Benjy rolling from the couch as though from the open door of an airplane. She remembers how even though she was older and knew better, she couldn't help but imagine her brother falling through a sea of smoke, disappearing finally, into the flames.

Fires of Our Choosing

WHEN LENNY'S HOUSE BURNED to the ground all I kept thinking was that it was just one more piece of bad luck in a life that had been full of it. Lenny was my best friend and over the years I had watched him drift from one misfortune to the next. He collected tough breaks the way other people collected sports memorabilia or antique furniture. Even his birth, fifteen years after his closest sibling's and obviously unplanned, must have seemed a superb misfortune to his parents, their child-rearing days so close to completion. He had emerged from the womb totally blind in his left eye, the blackness of his pupil leaking into his iris like spilled ink. Lenny had had it rough and he knew it, and I guess it was this that I liked best about him. I had known some hard times myself, and so commiserating with Lenny sometimes made me feel like we were the two lone survivors of a plane crash.

Lenny's parents had given him the house after they'd retired. They were sick of Erie's winters, so they bought a doublewide in some community down in Florida called *Pleasant Grove*, which Lenny called *Pleasant Grave* since he said people went there to die. After he helped them move, Lenny's parents signed the house's deed over to him. It was a modest three bedroom place that creaked when the wind blew and was badly in need of a new furnace, but the mortgage was almost completely paid off and it had a front porch where you could sit and drink a beer while watching a storm come in, so for the most part I had considered it a pretty righteous act of generosity.

I drove over the day after the fire and parked across the street from the rubble. The other houses that lined Lenny's block were plain two-story homes painted various shades of white or gray. They huddled close together in a row, the gap where Lenny's house used to stand like a single missing tooth. I found Lenny sifting through the remains, his clothes and face covered in soot. Even his blond hair was dark with ash. He looked like a homeless person, which I figured he was.

"Need some help?" I asked. I had a twelve-pack of Railbender with me and I set it down where his porch would have been.

Lenny stared for a second as if he didn't recognize me. It had been only a week or so since I'd seen him, but he looked like he'd lost weight. His face was drawn and his thin arms hung straight down at his sides. After a moment, something seemed to click.

"Eric," he said, shaking his head, "can you believe it?"

The truth was, I could believe it, but I wasn't about to tell that to Lenny. My normal policy for when something bad happened in his life was to lie. I would recite some generic saying meant to make him believe things would get better, that his life would not always be a series of tragedies connected by listless days working at his brother's plumbing company, a job he despised. "When life hands you lemons, make lemonade," I would say, or "That which does not kill us makes us stronger." Shit I didn't believe, but that sounded good enough to pass for sincere optimism. In turn, Lenny did the same for me, providing comfort with lies in the way that only a true friend can. Six months earlier he had come to the funeral home after my father's death and placed his hand on my shoulder. "You've handled yourself with a lot of dignity through all of this," he had said. He was wearing cowboy boots, a purple button-down shirt that was two sizes too big for him, and a clip-on tie. He looked ridiculous. "Your father would be proud of you." I had been drunk for two weeks straight, had received a DUI the morning after they took my father's body from our house. My mother had bailed me out of jail on her way to the funeral home to choose a casket. Dignity was a faraway country from which I had been exiled years before, a place I could hardly recall. But he had said those things to me regardless. It was our unspoken agreement. In comparison to all the other tragedies that had befallen Lenny over the years, this one reigned supreme. "I'm sorry about all this," I said, leaning toward the debris with my shoulder. "Just remember, after the storm comes the calm."

Lenny looked around like he was just noticing the charred remains for the first time. "That's right," he said. "Some calm would be nice right about now."

"Well it's on its way," I said, picking up the Railbender and moving toward him. "It's practically here already." The ground was covered with burnt wreckage making it hard to walk. "I brought you some beer."

"Thanks," Lenny said. After a moment he looked down at his wrist, at an imaginary watch, and said, "I guess it must be beer-thirty." This was something Lenny said a lot, but right then it didn't sound that funny.

I lowered the tailgate on Lenny's dented Ford Ranger. A black vinyl cover was snapped tight over the truck's bed, but with the tailgate down there was room to sit. Lenny turned the radio to the classic rock station. I handed him a beer and took one for myself.

"So what happened?" I asked.

Lenny drank half his beer in one big gulp, his Adam's apple bouncing in his throat.

"The fire inspector isn't sure yet, but I have my own theory."

"Which is what?"

"Arson," Lenny said.

"Who would set your house on fire?"

"I don't know," Lenny said. "That's what I've been trying to figure out." He set his beer on the tailgate and began to knead the back of his sunburned neck. Arson seemed far-fetched to me. In spite of all his bad luck, or maybe because of it, Lenny was a pretty likeable individual. He was the kind of guy who got along with most everyone. If he had enemies, I didn't know about them.

"Arson," I said, shaking my head.

Lenny looked at me in a serious way. He had two pinkish pockmarks from a teenage bout with the chickenpox on either side of his face, like permanent dimples.

"These things happen," he said apologetically, as though he was a teacher revealing one of the world's great injustices to his students. He finished his beer and threw the empty bottle toward the dirty remains of his house. "These things are not beyond the realm of possibility."

Lenny had not been home when the fire started. He had been eating chicken wings and drinking dollar drafts at the National Club, a bar he frequented over in Erie's Lower West Side. When he returned he found the house burning, a giant bonfire against the night sky. The firefighters informed him that it was beyond saving, that their only concern was to keep the fire from spreading. And so he stood there with his neighbors and watched his house burn.

"You have a place to crash?" I asked.

"I'm staying with Tiffany, out in Wattsburg." Tiffany was Lenny's sister. She had four kids by three different guys, and pretty much lived off the child support when the fathers actually paid it. Also, she grew pot behind her aboveground pool, a little piece of insider info that Lenny and I had occasionally abused. She'd gotten the house from her first divorce. I had only been inside once, but that was enough. Tiffany didn't have any pets but the place still managed to smell like cat piss and Lenny told me the sound of children crying was continuous, like a soundtrack that never ended. Plus, Wattsburg was the sticks and Lenny worked in town.

I tried to think of something to say. "At least you weren't in there." The blackened lump of the brick fireplace stood precariously like the primitive altar of some ancient tribe. "At least you're alive."

Lenny's face tightened in contemplation, as though he was considering, for the first time, his possible fate. His expression changed, the thought evaporating in his fury. "If I ever find the fuckers who did this," he said, "I'll burn *their* fucking house down."

Above us the sun was falling in the sky. A line of clouds stretched above it, their underside a brilliant orange. The air had cooled and felt good as it mixed with the heat that still seeped from the wreckage. A little ways down the street from Lenny's was a basketball court and I could hear the birthing of a pickup game: the hollow dribble of the ball, the rattle of the chain link fence that surrounded the court, the shit-talking already in full swing. I did not ask, but I knew that when I arrived Lenny was searching for anything that had survived the fire. Near the edge of his driveway was a small pile comprised of what he'd found: a remote control, a single candlestick, some of his parents' old vinyl 45s, hopelessly warped by the heat, and a pair of white Chuck Taylors yellowed by smoke. What remained of his life in a stack that anyone would have mistaken for trash. I put my hand on his shoulder. A breeze sent tiny pieces of ash dancing through the air like confetti. "You'll get through this," I said. "Better days will come."

Lenny looked at me with his sad, dead eye. "That's what you keep telling me."

After I left Lenny, I drove west across 26th Street past the off-ramps of I-79. A little farther on, the road widened and was flanked on both sides by a gray blur of abandoned warehouses and factories and then the shimmering oases of used car lots, their countless strings of tiny flags blowing furiously in the breeze like trapped kites. I took a right on Peninsula Drive. The after-work traffic had thinned out and with the roads almost empty I could go as slow as I wanted. The sun was nothing more than a thin crescent of orange above the blue of Lake Erie. I drove into its blinding glare not bothering to lower the visor. I couldn't get the image of Lenny covered in ash out of my head. We'd been friends since the third grade, playing basketball together, sleeping over at each other's houses, stealing cigarettes from his sister's purse. At first my parents treated him like another son, but by the time we reached high school they'd begun to dislike him. After graduation, Lenny took the job working for his brother, and I got accepted to a small college in Pittsburgh. It meant we wouldn't be hanging out much anymore, and although he didn't come right out and say it, I knew my father was happy. Pittsburgh wasn't far, just a hundred mile shot down I-79, but it was the first time I'd be living away from Erie, something I was pretty excited about. My parents helped me move down. While my mom was busy filling a dresser with neatly folded laundry, my father asked me to take a walk with him. We went down to the quad, a concrete courtyard surrounded by trees and benches. All around us the campus was alive with freshman carrying suitcases and boxes, trying their best to look cool in spite of the overeager parents trailing them.

We sat on a bench and my father straightened the collar of his blue Oxford. He was wearing beige khakis and white tennis shoes. He had been the first in his family to go to college and was now a well-regarded professor of American History at a Catholic university downtown. Khakis and tennis shoes were as casual as he got. The sun reflected off his bald head and his large eyebrows sloped in toward each other like they always did when he was thinking something over. Finally, he placed one of his big hands on my shoulder. "You'll do well here," he said, as if he had made up his mind and all that remained was to convince me. "This is a place where you can really thrive."

I had never been much of a student, never excelled at sports or art or music, but my father's faith in me had always been resolute. The worse I did, the more I disappointed him, the stronger it seemed to grow, as though he knew at any moment I would discover some ambition or talent hidden deep within and prove to the world that I was not just another fuck-up. My father, having always believed this to be the case, would be the first to congratulate me.

"Just study hard," he said, shaking me by the shoulder.

"I will," I said, trying my best to sound like I believed.

The complex where I lived was a group of single unit apartments built together in one low brown line, in the fashion of a cheap motel. The name of the place was Lakeview Vistas, although you could only see the lake on a clear day and even then it was just a thin strip of blue, out of place against the normally steel-gray sky. A concrete foundation ran along the front of the apartments and was used as a sort of makeshift porch. People set up small propane grills on top of card tables or arranged cheap mismatched patio furniture in front of their doors. I was somewhat of a hybrid between the complex's manager and its handyman, a position I fell into after failing out of college. I only lasted a semester and a half in Pittsburgh. Before long I was skipping class, spending entire days loafing around my dorm, high or hung-over or both, the kind of days where taking a shower could be viewed as an accomplishment. The job at the Vistas had seemed a wonderful stroke of luck to me after moving back home. My duties mainly consisted of collecting the rent checks and doing simple miscellaneous repairs. In return I received a free place to live and a small monthly stipend, not much but enough for food and beer. My parents were not as thrilled. When I came home I told them that the classes were too hard, that my professors didn't like me, that not everyone was cut out for college. But none of these reasons seemed to appease them in the same way they calmed me. My father insisted that the situation was temporary, that I was just taking a little time to get back on my feet before reapplying to school.

A couple of the tenants stood in the parking lot smoking and I nodded at them as I walked past. Most of the people who rented at Lakeview Vistas were transitory. The place was a revolving door for deadbeats and shit-heads and much of my job involved reminding people that their rent was past due, until finally they disappeared in the middle of the night, leaving me to plaster over the holes they punched in the drywall. Because of this I tried not to talk to anyone too much. Getting to know the other people who lived there only to have them leave unexpectedly made me feel like everyone else was moving on to bigger and better things. It made me feel stuck, and while I had agreed with my father, telling myself repeatedly that my time at the Vistas was limited, that it was just a stepping stone, three years had passed and I had begun to feel as much a part of the place as the ruptured blacktop of the parking lot or the outdated ice maker in the lobby that coughed out its crystal cubes like a slot machine.

The next morning I was cleaning out the gutters when the phone in my apartment rang. I waited, hoping whoever it was would just hang up, but when they didn't I climbed off the step ladder and went inside. Lenny was on the other end, breathing hard, his words coming in bursts.

"I know who it was."

"Who what was?"

"I know who burned my house down."

"Wait a second..."

"Meet me at the basketball courts by my house."

"I'm busy," I said. But it was too late. He had already hung up.

When I got to the courts I found Lenny sitting across the street in the Ranger with his window rolled down. He was smoking a cigarette and several spent butts lay on the asphalt below his door. I parked behind him and let myself into his truck.

"Aren't you supposed to be at work?"

Lenny was staring at a man playing basketball across the street. "This is more important than work," he said.

"What is?" I asked. "Watching some guy shoot around?"

"I'm doing surveillance," Lenny said, irritated. "Don't you see anything suspicious?"

"You mean *other* than you?"

"Seriously," Lenny said.

Across the street, a man wearing jean shorts and a dark tank top was lining up a shot from the foul line. He pushed the ball up awkwardly and it struck the rim with a thud. He walked over to collect his rebound before turning around. "Is that Ear-Dick?" I asked.

"Yep," Lenny said, obviously pleased.

Ear-Dick was a kid Lenny and I had gone to high school with. During the first week of freshman year, Ear-Dick was kneeling at his locker practicing his combination, when Joe Cilanso, a wrestler built like a nine-volt battery, approached. Ear-Dick didn't even have time to look up before Joe, who'd been hazing him since orientation, unzipped his pants and delivered one solid magnificent whack directly across his hearing canal. Joe was expelled, but for Ear-Dick it was too late, that swinging member cemented his rank in our school forever.

Lenny tapped his fingers against the steering wheel like he was typing. "Did you see his shoes?"

When I looked I recognized the yellowed Chuck Taylors Lenny salvaged from the fire.

"I forgot to take my stuff with me last night, and today it was all gone."

"You think Ear-Dick burned your house down for sneakers?"

"No, asshole," Lenny said. "But you remember what he was like back then, all weird and shit. Never talked, always by himself. I used to give him a hard time."

"Everyone gave him a hard time. For Christ's sake, we called him Ear-Dick. That doesn't make him an arsonist."

"You think it's just coincidence that my house burns down and the next day the weirdest kid in our high school is wearing my sneakers?" Dark patches sat below Lenny's eyes and his breath was heavy with the sweet warmth of alcohol. "It's all coming together. I told you I was going to find the fucker who did this," he said, and he smiled with satisfaction, like a man who'd won an argument. I could see that he really believed it. The sneakers, the timing, it was enough to go on, probably even more than he'd hoped for. "I bet he burned my house down for revenge," Lenny said. "And now I'm gonna fuck him up."

"He probably just walked by and thought they were trash."

"They're *not* trash," Lenny snapped. He opened the door and stumbled a little as he got out. He was wearing his work jeans and the same dirty AC/DC T-shirt as the day before. On the back of it, Angus Young decapitated someone with a bloody guitar.

"Hey," he yelled as he neared the courts. "Hey, Ear-Dick."

Ear-Dick was dribbling the ball, but when he heard Lenny shouting he stopped and looked up. After a moment he threw the ball in a haphazard way toward the rim and walked over to the side of the court where I finally caught up with Lenny.

"Hey, Lenny," he said. "Long time no see."

I was a little surprised that he remembered Lenny. After the incident freshman year, Ear-Dick disappeared into the nerdy abyss of AP science and Academic Sports League, graduating somewhere near the top of our class. Lenny and I took all regulars courses.

"How you been, Ear-Dick?" Lenny said.

"No one really calls me that anymore."

"Oh yeah, since when?"

"Since high school. That Ear-Dick shit was stupid kid stuff. A goof."

I knew Ear-Dick was struggling to keep his voice steady while maintaining eye contact, but with some guys acting tough just didn't come natural. Their tone was forced, sweat beaded along their brows, and they always looked away first. These were the guys you could tell were pretending from a mile away, and Ear-Dick was one of them.

He turned to me. "Hey, Eric, still hanging around with Lenny, huh?"

When he said this I felt even more ashamed than I already did. Standing there with Lenny on a basketball court in the middle of a workday, while he hassled some guy we hadn't seen since high school. I knew how pathetic it must have looked, and how it looked wasn't all that far from how it was.

My cheeks grew warm. "I guess so," I said. Somewhere down the block a car drove by blasting rap. The bass was so low I could feel it in my chest, thumping steadily like a second heartbeat. "What have you been up to?" I asked, trying to change the subject. Lenny was staring at him hard. His hands were at his sides, and he was opening and closing them like hungry little mouths.

"I'm taking summer classes at Slippery Rock," he said. "I'm six credits shy of a BS in business." He didn't say this in a condescending way, but sometimes the delivery doesn't matter. I thought of my own failed college career, how I didn't have six credits total.

"You hear that?" Lenny asked. "Ear-Dick is just six credits shy of a bullshit degree in business."

"It means Bachelor of Science," Ear-Dick said.

"I *say* it means bullshit," Lenny said, and when he did, Ear-Dick turned away. "If you're going to Slippery Rock, what're you doing back in Erie?"

"Visiting my parents. Is that *okay*?" He was facing me as he spoke.

"Where'd you get those sneakers?" Lenny asked.

Ear-Dick looked at the shoes. "I found them."

"More like you *stole* them."

"What are you talking about? I found them next to the dumpster on the corner," he said, pointing up the block, "piled with a bunch of other shit."

"It's not *shit*," Lenny said. He stepped forward.

"Come on, Lenny." I reached for his arm. "It wasn't him. Let's go."

Lenny pulled away. "It's my stuff," he said.

"What are you guys talking about?"

"Nothing," I said. "Forget it."

"You burned my house down."

"What?" Ear-Dick said. His face was pale and skinny with a chinstrap of zits stretching across his jaw line. I could tell he had no idea what we were talking about.

"Lenny's house burned down a few nights ago. He's just stressed out about it," I said, realizing how stupid it sounded.

Ear-Dick stood quietly for a moment letting the information settle. "Wow, Lenny, I'm sorry to hear that."

Lenny shifted his weight from one foot to the other. "No you're not."

"Yeah, you're right. I'm not."

Lenny hit him once. The punch caught Ear-Dick between his nose and lip with a sickening crack, and he went down where he stood. He didn't teeter or sway or stumble, he dropped, his legs giving way beneath him.

"What the fuck?" I said, taking a step back, putting some distance between myself and Lenny.

Lenny was standing over him breathing heavily as though he'd just sprinted around the court. "I knew it was him."

"It wasn't him."

"Are you kidding me? Of course it was." He said this like I was the crazy one. He still had his fists raised in a boxer's stance, as though at any moment Ear-Dick might jump up and fight back. Ear-Dick's chest rose and fell with the gentle rhythm of sleep. Other than that he was motionless, knocked out cold. His head was turned to one side and a puddle of blood was forming beside his face.

Lenny lowered his hands. After a moment he said, "We should go."

"We have to call an ambulance," I said. "We can't just *leave* him here."

"He's coming with us," Lenny said. He reached into his pocket and took out his keys.

"To a hospital?"

"After," Lenny said.

"After *what*?"

"After he admits what he did." Lenny said this like it was all very reasonable, like he half-expected me to be having the same train of thought.

"Are you retarded?"

Lenny's face tightened. His left hand was still balled into a fist. "Don't *say* that."

"It *wasn't* him," I said again. Cars whizzed by on 26th Street, and I worried that at any moment one of them would make a left turn and that whoever was inside would see us standing there, Ear-Dick sprawled on the pavement between us.

"You're supposed to be on *my* side," Lenny said. "You're supposed to believe *me*." He glared at me with his good eye. "*Please.*"

Behind him the basketball net swayed in the breeze. It had been a long time since I'd seen Lenny on a court. In junior high he'd been our team captain and MVP, fighting for rebounds under the boards, draining jumpers while his parents cheered from the stands. But at the first tryout in high school the coach took one look at Lenny's blind eye and put him on the practice squad. Lenny quit a week later. I thought about his house and how it was gone forever, nothing left but ashes and rubble and smoke-stained sneakers. I thought about how at the plumbing shop, his brother hired kids right out of high school to work on the jobsite and make union wages while Lenny still drove the supply van and took orders from guys who'd worked there half as long. I suddenly felt unsteady on my feet. I placed my hands on my thighs and leaned forward as Lenny's whole sad history unraveled itself before me.

"We'll just drive around till he wakes up. I'll ask him one more time, and then it's straight to the hospital. I swear." Lenny raised his hand as though taking an oath.

"Give me your keys," I said.

I pulled the truck over, and we undid the vinyl cover until it was halfway unfastened. We loaded Ear-Dick into the bed. The stream of blood had stopped flowing from his nose, as though whatever hidden source had fed it was now dry. We put him in on his side, wedging him between the wheel-well and a portable generator. We began to refasten the bed cover.

"What about air?" I asked. "How's he gonna breathe?"

"Relax," Lenny said. He shut the tailgate, unfastened a couple of the snaps that held the vinyl cover down, and pulled the loose corner back. "He'll be fine."

We went east on 26th Street until we reached Glenwood Park Avenue, which ran through my old neighborhood, a part of town I usually avoided. When Lenny turned right, headed away from the lake and out of town, we passed my old house, a red brick two-story, occupied now by some other family. The last time I was inside was two days before my father died. It was early in the morning. I had been driving around aimlessly all night, the cooler of beer beside me nearly empty, when I found myself in my parent's neighborhood. I had not intended to end up there. Hospice had been called in and their white van filled our driveway.

I found my mother and the hospice nurse keeping vigil beside my father's hospital bed. The only light came from a bedside lamp. The tubes that were attached to my father the last time I'd seen him were disconnected now.

"Where are his tubes?" I asked. Neither of them answered. They just left the room. I sat down in a chair next to the bed and watched as my father opened his eyes. When he saw me, he smiled, but I could tell that he was somewhere else, somewhere not in the room. Below his pale veiny skin, the cancer that had begun in his throat had travelled down the length of his chest and filled his stomach. It was eating everything that remained alive within him. He had been given a great deal of morphine, and his eyes looked huge and glassy.

"You're late," he said calmly. "Try to be on time from now on." His cheeks were sunken. Someone had tried to shave him, but areas of stubble remained here and there. I had never seen him with any facial hair and it surprised me how much it changed his appearance.

"Dad," I said. He was staring at a patch of nothing on the ceiling. I could tell he was about to say something.

"Did you know," he began, "that during the Revolutionary War, Benedict Arnold was shot in the leg while fighting for the Colonists?" He opened his eyes even wider and turned to me. "Did you know that?"

I shook my head, but he seemed not to notice.

"He was crippled for the rest of his life, but people only remember him as a traitor."

"Dad," I repeated. There was something I needed to say, something I had not yet found the words for.

"That's the way history works," he said. "That's the way the world works." He turned back toward the ceiling and took a deep breath. My own breath caught in my chest. Across the room, the first light of the day streamed pale yellow through the drawn beige curtains. "After the Doolittle Raid on Tokyo, the Japanese military killed 250,000 Chinese civilians. They did that because the Chinese were helping downed American Airmen." He began to move his hand about before him. "It's extraordinary," he said. "The Chinese didn't even know us, but they helped. Does anybody know how extraordinary that is?" His eyes searched the ceiling, following the direction of his finger, pointed in front of him. I knew then where he was, standing at the front of his classroom, leading his students, offering them the inexplicable acts of men and scanning the desks for answers, for a raised hand, for anything. His eyes passed over my face as they might have passed over any student's. "People do extraordinary things every day," he said.

"Dad," I said. He stopped pointing and for a moment I thought that he'd heard, that he was back in the room. He let his hand fall onto his blanket, and his glazed eyes fixed on me and what I wanted to tell him was that I was sorry, for everything, that I was a fuck-up and I knew it but I could change, that it wasn't too late for me to change. I wanted to beg him to forgive me. I wanted to thank him for always believing, for not giving up on me when anyone else would have. That's what I wanted to tell him, but I didn't. Instead, I lowered my head and heard myself say, "Please stop expecting anything from me." When I raised my head his face held a serious expression, his eyebrows sloped toward each other.

"You remind me of my son," he said. He seemed to be studying me, searching my features, and then suddenly his expression twisted until I thought he might cry out. "*Ohhh*," he said, and I wasn't sure if he said it from pain or sadness or if there was any difference at all.

Lenny and I took the low road out of Erie. Once we passed the city limits Lenny opened the glove box and pulled out a pint of Beam and we passed it back and forth until we drained the color from it. We smoked cigarettes and we took our time. There was nowhere we needed to be and no real hurry to get there. The farther away from the lake we drove the more confusing the roads became, two lane highways that cut through pastures and around dairy farms and circled in every direction and sometimes back into themselves. Even if you'd lived there all your life, you could get lost. We passed Summit and Waterford and Mill Village, towns so small they were easy to miss. Every now and then we passed a one pump gas station, or a farmhouse or grain silo set back from the highway, or an isolated brick building advertising deer processing. Other than that there was nothing, just the fields and the horizon and the road that connected them.

"We should head out to Wattsburg," Lenny said, "to my sister's place. We'll be safe there until Ear-Dick wakes up."

I nodded and Lenny used an emergency pull off to start a U-turn. He knew the back roads better than I did and fifteen minutes later we were rocking slightly over the long gravel driveway that led to Tiffany's house.

A thin cut of woods shielded the house from view and when we emerged from it the front yard spread before us. It was different than the last time I was there; now it was filled with every type of lawn ornament and decoration imaginable. Tiny working windmills, gazing balls, a granite fountain continuously filled by a peeing cherub, lawn jockeys, wheelbarrows and giant tires full of flowers, along with countless other figures, covered nearly every available inch of grass. It was as though the sky opened and shat a great mass of junk into her front yard. Among these decorations were children, two or three live children, who seemed to note our arrival with cautious interest, peeking out at us from their camouflaged vantages. Tiffany stood next to the wide porch.

In one hand she held a cigarette and in the other the hand of a small girl wearing only a diaper. When she saw us pull up she started to walk over, still holding the little girl's hand as she dodged the obstacles in her way. She was moving fast and the little girl kept falling down. The first few times Tiffany hoisted her back to her feet but finally she abandoned the effort and left her lying on her stomach next to a tiny ceramic gnome.

"Where have you *been*?" Tiffany screamed as she approached the truck. Lenny cringed. She was a big woman, tall and curvy and loud. She was wearing a white blouse and a pair of gray sweatpants with Mickey Mouse ears stitched onto the pockets. Among the clutter of the yard, two little boys stumbled upon one another and began to fight with plastic swords. One had a curly mess of red hair and the other a blond crew cut that made him appear bald. They looked nothing alike.

When Tiffany reached the open window of the truck she was breathing hard. "I've been calling your cell all day," she said. Her big fat face seemed to take up the whole window.

"Hey," I said, but she ignored me. Across the yard the red-haired boy knocked down the blond one and stripped him of his weapon. The boy on the ground seemed to beg for mercy, but the red-haired boy kicked him in the stomach instead.

"Fire inspector called here looking for you," Tiffany said.

"What'd he want?" Lenny said.

"To tell you how the fire got started, retard."

Lenny cringed again.

"He traced it to the stovetop. Apparently someone left the burner going when he went to the bar. Wonder who that could've been?" Tiffany's thin colorless lips formed a faint smile, as though she found some pleasure in this sudden turn of events. At that moment, I hated her.

"You," she said, "burnt down Mom and Dad's house." She raised her finger and pointed it right in Lenny's face. "*You*," she repeated. There was a finality in her voice that scared me, like a judge sentencing a prisoner.

"I hardly ever use the stove," Lenny said, as though this completely absolved him. "It couldn't have been me."

"Hardly's got nothing to do with it. They found a greasy pan on the stove and everything. What'd you do, get drunk and try and make something?" Lenny's good eye flashed with some sort of recognition. "Now you've really done it." Across the yard, the red-haired boy kicked his brother again and this time the boy cried out in pain. Tiffany turned around. "Enough," she yelled. "Leave your brother alone." She gave Lenny one more disgusted look and then moved toward the screaming child.

Lenny put the truck in drive and hit the gas. He spun the wheel hard and the back tires sprayed dirt. Tiffany's curses filled the cab even after we pulled out onto Route 8.

Lenny was driving scary fast. I reached over and grabbed at my seatbelt, but there wasn't one so I just held on. Cornfields and pastures flew past in a green blur. My window was down and the noise the truck made as it cut through the air was deafening. Lenny's knuckles were white on the wheel. The veins in his neck bulged and seemed to pulse. The needle on the speedometer crept past eighty.

"I don't care what she says. It wasn't me."

Outside the light was beginning to fail, throwing shadows across the road that looked like oil stains. A hazy purple hue covered everything. I thought about Ear-Dick, bloody and unconscious, wedged in the bed of the truck. I knew that by waiting, we were making decisions that could not be undone. I thought about my father, how he never approved of Lenny, how happy he was when I left for school. Lenny was concentrating hard on the road, half blind and stone-faced. A line of stratus clouds stretched beyond the windshield like a second horizon, a thin violet bruise below the setting sun. The fields rolled away in low swells toward distant tree lines. We passed a dirt service road and an abandoned gas well set back from the highway, and I realized that I had no idea where we were, that this was a place I had never been to. All I knew was that we were far from home, that even if we turned around right then, the trip back would be long.

Lenny lifted his hand and hit the steering wheel once, hard. "I can't believe she said it was *me*." His voice sounded desperate, as though he was pleading. The landscape continued to reveal itself: tilled earth, green fields, a flock of starlings peppering the sky, all of it unfamiliar, the world humming with newness. We'd come too far to do anything but keep going.

I waited until Lenny returned my stare. "You shouldn't believe everything you hear," I said. "Consider the source."

After a moment, he began to nod. "That's right," he said. "What does she know? She's been jealous ever since Mom and Dad gave me the house." He eased his foot off the accelerator.

"Exactly," I said.

Lenny loosened his grip on the wheel, lowered himself in his seat. "I just wish things would look up," he said. "I wish for that a lot."

"I do too," I said, "but remember, it's always darkest before the dawn."

We continued on like that for a long time, the highway disappearing beneath us as we passed through towns named Cutting and Corry and Spartansburg. Dusk gave way to nighttime. We didn't talk anymore. We just drove silently with the radio off, not thinking of our pasts or our futures, or the boy in the back of the truck and how he might come to factor into them. We just kept driving, listening to the wind as it rushed over the hood of the truck. Now and again, it came across the highway, pulling us toward the center line or else toward the ditch at the edge of the field. Lenny tightened his grip on the wheel and did his best to keep us steady, but we both knew there was only so much you could do, that at any moment that wind could sweep you off the road, or else the earth could open up and swallow you whole, that in the end it was all beyond our control, and in this we found comfort.

Come August

COMB THE TANGLES from the neighbor girl's hair being careful not to tug too hard. You don't want her telling her mom, who's good friends with your mom, that you're a bad sitter.

Let the sun bronze your back and think about Jason. Last night at the bonfire, did he look at Lauren the way he used to look at you? Promise yourself not to care, then break that promise all day long.

Keep an eye on your sister as she chases Einstein across the dry grass, swatting at his tail. Already you feel the neighbor girl pulling away, her tiny body straining to break free. You let her go and she runs down the slope of the yard, arms flailing like she's on fire. Watch her shadow your sister, who at three is a few months older and the leader. In the summer, when you're there to babysit, they spend every day together. It's the middle of June and already they can't stand to be apart. Watch them disappear into the playhouse with Einstein trailing them, the glutton for punishment that he is. They swing the door shut behind them.

Far below you, at the edge of your yard is the pond your

stepfather built and stocked with bass. It's the hottest day of the year and you wish your mom was here to watch the girls so you could have a swim. Stare hard enough at the short wooden pier and it seems to sway. Sometimes you sit there at night, your feet invisible below the dark water, and stare at the sky, imagining yourself in other places. Be grateful you don't live in the city. In the city you're never alone.

Ignore the pounding in your head and check your phone for missed calls. Nothing. It's almost noon. Four hours until your mom gets home and you're free. Four hours until your real day begins. The girls toddle out of the playhouse bare-chested and giggling wildly. A moment later Einstein walks out with two pink tank tops stretched taut across his long brown body. They have dressed him before, in skirts and scarves and printed T-shirts. But still, he comes out looking surprised, red eyes wide, ears straight up, as though he was not expecting this.

Dress the squirming girls and lead them inside through the open garage for lunch. Close the back door behind you and feel the cooler air cover your skin. In the kitchen, make two PB & Js with your grandma's strawberry preserves and cut off the crusts. It's still too hot to eat and the girls make excuses before you finally give in and hand them each a push pop from the freezer. Smile when they hug your legs with the type of gratitude that only little kids can show and then watch as they paint their faces a sticky orange.

Look, Megan, the neighbor girl says smiling. *Lipstick.*

Throw the barely touched sandwiches in the trash and take the girls back outside. Make them stand there while you rub suntan lotion onto their warm skin. They are both fair and will burn easily so use the SPF 40. Set them free and check your phone again. Forget the fact that your ringer is loud and you would have heard any call. Stare at the blank screen and drink your water. Last night, along with the keg that is always sitting in someone's trunk at the bonfires, there was jungle juice, a punch so sweet you could hardly believe there was any liquor in it, which is why, maybe, you drank so much, and now your brain is drowning in your skull. When it was time to leave, you stumbled a little. Hope that Jason did not see.

Watch the girls play house, holding hands and pushing a double stroller as they imitate what they imagine to be a perfect family. After your father left, your mother remarried and you were happy for her. Your stepfather is a good man and though you are not his own daughter, he treats you as if you were. And so you were happy also when your mother kept the promise she made him, that they would have a child together. And though your sister is really your half-sister, you never think of her as half anything. At the end of the summer, when you leave for school, you'll miss her. The way she climbs in bed with you on Sunday mornings, the way that sometimes, if she wakes up in the night crying from a bad dream, she asks to see you. Look at her now and notice again those parts you've both inherited from your mother. The straw blond hair that curls loosely in the heat, the rounded cheeks you resent, but which make her even cuter. Once, when she asked why you had different dads, you told her it didn't matter, that you were different versions of the same song. She is a part of you and you will miss her when you leave, but not enough to stay.

Try and remember how far Ann Arbor is from Waterford. Something like three hundred miles. Imagine again the people you will meet there. In your mind you've already created your group of friends and lived out in a blur the new life that will begin with them, the new life that will begin come August. You will share a house together your sophomore year. You will throw parties where everyone dresses in pajamas. You will tailgate for football games and stay up late watching movies and go to the library to meet boys. You will forget the names of those boys who hurt you in your previous life.

The housing department sent you a letter that said your roommate's name is Isabella. Smile when you imagine her, exotic and tall and sweet. She will invite you home with her over breaks to visit her family, in California or Spain.

Hold the cool water bottle to your head and count slowly to ten. From your pocket comes a muffled beep. Check your phone. One new text. From Jason. *I've been thinking about you.* Close the phone. He's been thinking about a lot of girls. Try and guess how many messages like this one he's sent out today. Which number are you? Don't be the one who writes back.

Watch your sister blow bubbles while the neighbor girl tries to catch them. Watch them pop in her tiny hands like something that was never there. Remember the afternoon you told your mother you were going camping with friends. When she finally agreed you drove straight to Jason's. You left your car there and he took you to his parents' cottage at Findley Lake. Of all the nights in your entire life, this is the one you think of the most. A day has not passed since that you have not replayed every detail in your mind. Remember the smell of cedar. Remember the wine you drank, Boone's Farm, warm and sweet. Remember how he said everyone in Waterford felt the same to him. Everyone but you. Afterwards you washed the sheets in the bathtub while he slept, and then watched him, his tan chest rising and falling along with some inaudible rhythm you believed you were now a part of. You climbed into bed beside him and in his sleep he put his arm over you and you thought, *So this is what it feels like to be in love.* In the morning you kissed him awake and as soon as he opened his eyes you could tell. Remember how cool he acted as he drove you away from the cottage. Beside you a thick fog was rising from the water, vanishing in the air like a dream upon waking, and you thought, *That is me, from this day on, that is the way I will always be.* Remember how his mother stared at you from behind a curtain as you pulled away from his house, like you were a thief, like you were the one who had stolen something.

Watch the girls chase each other, running in circles until they drop. Usually by now they would be fading, draining themselves steadily until a nap was inevitable, but not today. Today they are relentless, like the heat.

In the distance you can hear the rush of traffic sailing along Route 19. Sometimes it feels like everyone is going somewhere. It's moments like that when you hate to be still. Lick the sweat from your upper lip, a taste like an overripe apple. Resolve to give the girls ten more minutes before their afternoon nap, then wait fifteen. Step off the porch and walk down to the yard inconspicuously, like you're lost. Avoid eye contact but watch the girls, note their location. Of course they spot you right away and, knowing why you're really there, they run. Give chase until you have the both of them, laughing and squirming frantically under each arm like fish. Walk them up the slope of the yard and set them down. Take their hands and lead them sulking through the open garage.

In your sister's room you begin to prepare the crib when you feel a tug on your shorts. It's your sister wearing her pretty-please face. *No Megan, Bunchy Bunchy*, she says. Bunchy Bunchy is what she calls it when you make her a bed on the floor. And since you are happy just to be inside away from the heat, you start to build her one. First her comforter, then a sheet and blanket, then pillows, and finally a tiny army of stuffed animals around the perimeter for protection. Lay her down in the middle and put the neighbor girl beside her. Tell them they must be lucky girls, to get to have a sleepover in the middle of the day. Put on their favorite movie and turn the sound down low. *Snow White*. The same movie you'd watch twice a day when you were little. Watch as the screen fills with the castle you once dreamed of living in. Even then you imagined there must be more to the world than what you could see. Brush the hair away from your sister's eyes. You say, *Rain, rain*, and she says, *go away*, and you both laugh because it is a joke that only the two of you share. Kiss her and the neighbor girl and switch off the light. Leave the door open a crack. If they need you, they'll know they can call out and you will hear. Listen to them giggle as you walk down the hall. Hope the movie settles them until sleep takes hold.

Walk past your room and notice the boxes standing in the corner. Orientation is still sixty-four days away, but already you've begun to pack. Already you've decided what you will take and what you will leave behind.

Settle into the living room couch. The clock on the stereo reads quarter till three. A little over an hour and your mom will be there to relieve you. A little over an hour until your real day begins.

Turn on the TV and flip through the channels. This time of day there's nothing on but soaps and infomercials and fake judges. A breeze pushes through the screened window across the room and brushes you as it goes past. You overdid it last night, intentionally or not, and now you are fighting to stay awake. Check the time again. Just an hour to go. Close your eyes and feel the pain in your head soften; the lack of light, the nearness of sleep, either way it's a refuge. Keep your eyes closed and remember what somebody once told you, that Michigan in the fall is like no place else on earth.

Awaken to the sound of Einstein barking in the distance, the way he does when he is worrying a rabbit or a squirrel.

Rub your eyes and when the black spots form, follow them as they dance along the walls. Lift yourself up and shake the sleep from your skinny limbs. The clock on the stereo reads quarter till four. A light at the end of your tunnel.

Walk with measured steps to your sister's bedroom. If the girls are still sleeping you will let them be until your mom gets home. It is too hot and you are too tired to watch them anymore.

Run your fingers along the wall. Listen to the music coming through it. A song that makes you feel safe. Take another step and see that the door is open. Walk in and find the bed you made deserted, occupied only by dolls. Call out your sister's name. Call out the neighbor girl's name. Probably they are hiding, peering through the slats of the closet or from underneath the crib as they try hard not to giggle.

Call them again, this time with anger. Switch off the movie and listen for their breathing, as soft as a breeze through leaves. But you don't hear it. Search the room and find nothing. Walk out into the hall and call them again. Say, *You are both in big trouble, I mean it.* And you do. When they finally produce themselves you will scold them for scaring you. Check your room, your parents' room, the kitchen, the couch. Find nothing. Walk outside through the open garage. Let the sunlight blind you, the heat attack your skin. When the black spots have faded from your vision, check the playhouse, the swing set. Nothing. Kneel down and look beneath the porch. Black and dusty and bare. Listen again and hear the only thing you've been hearing all along. Einstein. Still worrying over something. Still barking away.

Stand and search until you see him, a brown speck at the end of the pier, jerking his body toward the pond with each bark. Beyond him the water is white where the sunlight touches it. Watch the pier as it seems to sway. Somewhere above you a cloud covers the sun. Watch as two pink specks appear on the water where before there was only white.

Run down the hill toward the pond. Move as fast as you can and let gravity do the rest. Reach the edge and throw your long body out over the water.

Years from now, long after your mother finds you, incoherent, the two girls held limp at your sides, long after the paramedics leave, their presence pointless but obligatory, long after the police arrive and ask their questions and some of them, grown men, strangers, see what has happened and break down, long after the lawsuits and the newspaper articles and the funeral you are banned from attending, long after you see something vanish from your stepfather's eyes that will never return, long after you have asked your mother for the millionth time if she's forgiven you, and for the millionth time she lies, long after you realize that you will never overcome this day, that it will remain the event that defines you, long after all of that, when it seems like something that happened in another lifetime, or something that happened yesterday, you will understand this: a part of you never left that pond, never crawled soaking through the mud, screaming as you tried to put back life where there was no life left.

Fall underneath the water and open your eyes. Let the cool surround you. Let it dissolve the heat of the day. And though you don't mean to, for a moment, you imagine what you have been imagining all summer, that when you swim up for air you will break the surface of some calm lake in Michigan. It will be fall and the trees that surround the water will be filled with fierce shades of yellow and orange and red. On shore your new friends will be standing near a campfire, its smoke twisting loosely into the air. You will hear them calling to you as you tread water. For a moment you will be still. The brisk air will feel good as it brushes against your face and you will watch as the clouds above you float through a sky that's bluer than any you have ever seen. Your friends will call to you again, their collective voice echoing out across the water. Watch them waving, asking you to join them. And when you are finally ready, turn and level your body, and begin the long swim that will lead you to shore.

Only the Strong Will Survive

ON THE LAST SATURDAY in April, I take Meredith to El Canelo, a new Mexican restaurant downtown, where I'll ask her for the second time if she will marry me. I've reserved a table in the corner, and I tip the hostess when she seats us, coolly slipping a neatly folded five into her palm as though this is something I do often. I order chicken flautas and carne asada and fried ice cream, thanking our waiter in Spanish with each dish he brings. A three-man mariachi band stops at our table and serenades us, playing "Spanish Eyes," which I have requested. And although Meredith is second-generation Polish American and has pale blue eyes, the song seems to strike some chord within her, and she rubs my foot with hers beneath the table. She has settled comfortably into the evening, and it seems to me that she doesn't suspect another proposal. So after the band moves on and both our minds are sufficiently eased by the frozen peach margaritas we've been drinking, I lower myself onto one knee, and under the amber glow of a neon Dos Equis sign, its constant buzzing somehow reassuring, I ask her if she will be my wife. The ring, I tell her, as I told her the first time, is hers to pick out when she agrees. I watch from my lowered position as Meredith looks up, meeting the gaze, I'm sure, of the restaurant's other occupants, who are probably all looking at us by now.

"Oh, Ronny," she says, gushing, "you are such a sweetheart." She smiles, her face softly lit by the hanging advertisement for imported beer. And then when the waiting and the romance and the pain of the ceramic floor tile digging into my knee are all so immense I feel I might burst, she leans close and whispers into my ear, "But no. I'm sorry."

Deflated, I lift myself up, lean forward, and kiss her anyway. I can feel the eyes of the other diners fixed on my every move like laser sights. When I sit down, Meredith takes my left hand and gives it a squeeze, then dips a tortilla chip into a clay dish of pico de gallo. She explains that her reason for not marrying me hasn't changed. It's the same one she gave me in the middle of the Glenwood Ice Skating Rink, where I proposed to her for the first time two months ago on Valentine's Day.

"It's Joey," she says.

Joey is Meredith's son. He's fourteen, a karate novice, and the wrench in my wedding plans. He's a pudgy boy with braces and a tangled mess of black curls, and he doesn't like me at all. Usually I attribute Joey's dislike of me to jealousy. Maybe he thinks I'm trying to take his mother from him, although it's hard to imagine anyone taking Meredith some place she wasn't ready to go. Or perhaps it's simply teen angst. But I could just as easily attribute his dislike of me to genetics, since his father, Joey Sr., was a high school classmate of mine and didn't like me either. Joey Sr., with his crew cut and powerful limbs like sacks of concrete, was a heavyweight wrestler and fullback for the football team. He called me Bonny and Bitch Cakes and Fuck Monkey and would shove me into lockers, hold my head under the water fountain, or give me Indian burns until the skin of my forearms turned raw. He married Meredith, who attended an all-girl Catholic high school across town, the summer after we all graduated and Joey Jr. was born before Christmas arrived. Two years later Joey Sr. broke his hand punching a wall and ran away with the technician who took his x-ray at St. Vincent's, the same hospital where Meredith worked as a candy striper, where she is now a nurse. Meredith and I met on a blind date three years ago, and have been together since. But Fairview, the township where we live, is small and I knew who her ex-husband was and when I told her how he'd treated me in high school, she put two and two together.

"Wait a second. You're Fuck Monkey?" she'd asked.

"Used to be."

"He was such an asshole," she'd said. "I always told him not to pick on people."

"That was a long time ago," I had told her then. But sometimes, even now, it doesn't feel that long ago at all.

The mariachi band has retired for the night and the only sound now is a low chatter coming from the few remaining tables. Meredith tries to feed me a chip but I keep my mouth closed like a baby refusing his food.

"Come on now. Let's not let this spoil our evening."

I've already paid the check and am ready to leave. I push my chair back from the table and stand up.

"Joey," I say, "spoils everything."

The next day I drive to the taxidermy store I own, Custom Critters, to finish mounting an eight-point buck. Custom Critters is a small space located all the way at the end of the Imperial Street Strip Mall. Next to Meredith, taxidermy is my great love. When I was younger, my father practiced taxidermy as a hobby. He used to take me hunting and let me watch him work on the animals in our garage. I had a great respect for these animals, the way they had adapted and evolved and managed to survive for so long, not only from hunters but from predators in the wild. When I would explore the woods near our house, I tried to imagine that I was seeing things as a deer might, alert and swift in my reactions. I would stand in the middle of the trees and leaves and underbrush, the forest floor soft below my hiking boots, and listen for any noise I couldn't recognize. It was at these times, watching the sunlight spill through the canopy of trees, that I felt most at peace in the world.

After I graduated, I went to a school in Duluth specializing in taxidermy and then came home to open my own store. In the beginning, I was excited about the location. A two-lane highway runs beside the strip mall, so I put up a sign on the side of my shop facing it, hoping it might interest people to come in and see what taxidermy is all about. Like myself, people still hunt in Fairview. They sit in tree stands and drink during deer season, and set box traps for small game along the muddy banks of Walnut Creek. But something has changed from when I was young; a pride that was once there is gone. Fathers no longer care about mounting their sons' first deer, and sons don't seem to mind. The only concern anymore is having the animal processed so the meat can be carried home in large cardboard freezer boxes. It seems now that people only pass my storefront on their way home from the mall, after they've already bought their greeting cards, or eaten at the Chinese buffet, or had their hair styled at Max's Salon.

I display all the animals I have for sale in the showroom up front and do my work in a small square room in back. Being by myself there, working on my animals in silence,

I get that same sense of peace I did as a boy standing alone in the woods. In the center of the room is my stainless steel work table and I uncover the deer head lying on it. I carefully brush the smooth hair, feeling its velvet softness beneath my fingertips. There are some animals that I have invested so much of myself in that I can't imagine ever selling them. I've already preserved the buck's head and stained its antlers, and all that remains is to attach the mount to a solid oak trophy panel. Just as I'm about to begin, the phone rings. When I answer I hear Meredith's voice on the other end, sharp and angry.

"Did you forget what today is?"

"No," I say. I wait and all I get is silence. "Maybe."

"Today is Sunday, Ronald," she says. I know when she calls me Ronald that I'm in trouble. Ronny is reserved for when she feels affectionate. Other than that it's just plain Ron.

"Sunday," she says again to jar my memory.

"Sunday," I repeat, searching.

"I told you last week that Sunday was Joey Jr.'s tae kwon do test."

I don't remember her telling me this. It's a very real possibility she mentioned something and I forgot, or never heard at all. Sometimes when we argue on the phone, usually about Joey, I'll hold the receiver down by my waist and listen to the continuous buzzing of her voice. After she slows or stops altogether I'll put the phone back to my ear and say something like "Sorry," or, "You're right, honey," or sometimes, when I'm feeling daring, I'll say, "I just don't know." She might have told me about the tae kwon do test during one of these times. I just don't know.

"Joey Jr. is going for his brown belt," Meredith is saying. "This is a big deal." Meredith is very close to her son. She dotes on him. For instance, after karate class on Tuesday and Thursday nights she will drive him first to Burger King for a Whopper and then to Taco Bell for a Soft Taco Supreme, rather than just having him choose one place or the other. This is the kind of mother she is, strict but accommodating.

"It's too late for you to pick us up," she says. "Meet us at the dojo."

The dojo is a small brick building near the airport with an apartment built onto the side of it. On the front there is a hand-painted sign that reads *Steve's House of Karate* with a golden cobra curling out of the *e* in *Karate*. Inside, the floor is pinewood covered with a thick layer of wax. The whole place smells sourly of feet. The testing has already begun so I find Meredith in the back and sit in the plastic chair she's saved.

"Joey hasn't gone yet," she whispers. Her breath is warm against my ear. Waiting in her chair she looks pretty, but anxious. The same way she always does. Her thick black hair is pinned up, revealing the soft curve of her pale shoulders. She has a nice full figure and sometimes when I catch her coming out of the shower, I admire her shape, the way her hips widen roundly from her torso.

She's bouncing her knee nervously, and I rest my hand on it to try and calm her. After a while Joey Jr. emerges from a side door leading to the changing area. He's wearing his karate uniform, white pants and a white jacket closed in the front with a white belt, all of it made from a heavy starched material that creases like folded typing paper when he moves.

"He looks like the Stay Puft Marshmallow Man," I whisper to Meredith, who shushes me.

Joey Jr. moves onto a large rectangular red mat in the center of the room. He looks nervous. Behind him the wall is covered with mirrors that stretch from the floor to the ceiling. Steve, the karate instructor, is a muscular black man with long, dreadlocked hair. He places a large, powerful hand on Joey's shoulder.

"Ladies and gentlemen, this is Joey Mason and he is going for his brown belt. The first part of his test is a *kata*. This is a pattern of strikes, kicks, and attack poses that Joey has memorized. Joey, are you ready?"

Joey nods and everyone claps. After bowing to his instructor and the audience, Joey begins to move. Slowly he lifts his arms and opens his palms. With his hands, he makes rounded circles in the air around his body. He lifts his legs, stepping slowly at first, and then faster, from one end of the mat to the other. Then he rotates until his back is to us and we can only see his face in the mirrors, and then suddenly, he twirls around and moves toward us chopping precisely with outstretched hands. It's the most graceful thing I have ever seen him do. Usually he lies on the couch in Meredith's living room, playing video games, not caring that his t-shirt rises above his flour-sack stomach. Here his movements are fluid, one leading into the next as if this whole crazy punching and kicking exhibition was some dance he'd been practicing alone in his bedroom for months. By the time he's done, the nervousness has vanished from his face and his blue eyes shine with pride. He stops and bows at Steve and then us. Meredith is clapping before anyone else, her hands coming together as if to attack one another. Steve moves next to Joey Jr. on the mat.

"Excellent. For the final part of the test I need a volunteer to help Joey demonstrate his self-defense maneuver." For a few moments the room is quiet. The men are looking straight ahead trying not to draw attention to themselves, and it's clear that no one really wants to volunteer. But then, before

I can stop her, Meredith hoists my arm up in the air like the disjointed limb of a marionette.

"Here," she says. "Right here, Sensei Steve. Ronald volunteers."

Steve looks at me relieved. The rest of the audience turns to me and applauds my seeming courage, and by then it's too late. If I refuse now, Meredith will be embarrassed, and after some prodding by Steve someone else will step forward and volunteer in my place, and I will catch hell about it for at least a month. I weave my way through the audience and before I step on the mat, Steve tells me I must remove my boots. I lower myself slowly until I'm sitting cross-legged on the wooden floor. The laces are long and tied twice around the ankle. It takes me some time and I can feel everyone watching and waiting as though I'm the one being tested. When I step onto the mat, I can see that Joey Jr. is even less pleased by my being there than I am. His thin lips are curled apart revealing the slight metallic flash of low-end orthodontics and making his teeth look as if they were made of sharp metal. His ears are as small and flushed as candied plums, and his dark eyebrows are slightly raised. To someone else he might appear surprised or fairly bored. But I can interpret this look. It's reserved solely for me, to be suffered alone. I've never seen him give it to anyone else. And behind it there is the faintest trace of confident anticipation, as if he is privy to the future and is pleased by what he sees.

"The name of this maneuver is a *Go no sen*," Steve says. The way he pronounces this is intimidating, like he's spitting out glass. "All I need you to do is take a step forward and grab Joey's wrist."

I give him a wry smile. "Easy for you to say." Nobody laughs. Joey has already assumed his attack pose. His feet are spread apart and facing outwards and his hands are waist high and ready to strike. I bow to him as I've seen Steve do, and he leans down slightly, obviously impatient with the formality. I take a step toward him and wrap my fingers around his soft, white wrist. Instantly Joey traps my hand with his free one, and pulls me toward him. Before I can retreat, I'm sailing around his body like a ballroom dancer, his hip catapulting me through the air. I land on my back with a hollow thud, the wind knocked out of me. I hear a woman in the audience, not Meredith, gasp. Joey hovers above me, his left foot raised in the air as if he's contemplating putting a mens'-size-eleven hole through my chest, and ending my pathetic existence forever. I'm trying to choke down some air, but my throat feels like it's sealed shut. Joey lowers his foot and bows to me and then the audience. There is an explosion of applause, Meredith's clapping rapid and distinguishable from the rest. I think of how these people shower this little maniac with accolades, and then in twenty years they'll scratch their heads and wonder why he became a serial killer.

When I'm finally able to breathe again, I sit up and smile for everyone, the same way I used to smile after Joey Sr. would de-pants me in the lunchroom. It's a defiant sort of smile, one meant to repel pity. At first it feels strange on my face, but then it settles in naturally. I haven't used it in some time and I resent having to now. I stand and go to put my boots back on, but before I can Steve reminds me that I must bow to my opponent. And when I turn around I see Joey waiting for me to do so, unable to hide his pleasure. We lean toward each other, and suddenly I am afraid that my back will lock up forcing me to remain in this pose of submission forever. I think about rearing back and landing a ferocious kick underneath his plump, hairless chin, just to see how he likes being hurt and humiliated in front of a roomful of strangers. But instead I straighten up and walk back to my seat.

Afterwards, in the parking lot, Joey and Meredith walk in front of me, talking excitedly and looking at the certificate he's been given. It's nothing more than a piece of parchment paper, made to look old, with his and Steve's signatures on the bottom. In a few months it will be forgotten at the bottom of a drawer in Joey's bedroom, but for now it's all they can focus on. I reach to grab Joey by the shoulder to get his attention, but think better of it and call his name.

"You didn't have to flip me so hard," I say. Joey and Meredith both turn around to face me, and at once I realize I'm outnumbered.

"What are you talking about?" he asks, like an innocent little prick.

I know it's stupid of me to complain, but I can't help it. "You didn't have to throw me full force like that," I say. "I have a bad back you know."

"I think you're overreacting," Meredith says.

"You would," I tell her, and I feel like a child bringing up something that happened a long time ago and doesn't matter anymore.

"It was just a part of his test," she says.

I expect Joey to say something like "You're not my father," or "I don't have to listen to your shit." But instead he says, "Only the strong will survive, Ronald."

It's something his father used to say at pep rallies before big games or after he'd knock the books out of my hands in the hallway. The thought occurs to me that without ever really knowing his father, the odds are that Joey Jr. will turn out to be exactly like him.

"Has it ever occurred to you that you're a complete asshole?" I ask him.

"*Ronald*," Meredith says, shocked.

"Better than being a complete pussy," Joey says.

"Get in the car right this minute," Meredith tells him. She knows this was bound to happen. He and I have come to words before. Our mutual dislike can only simmer for so long.

Joey Jr. gives me one more menacing glance and then climbs into the back of their minivan, sliding the door shut behind him. Meredith is giving me a disapproving stare.

"*What?*"

"You would think that with you being the closest thing he has to a father figure, you'd be a little more patient with him."

"He's a carbon copy of his father and he'll probably turn out to be just as big a dickhead." After it's out, I realize that at a crucial juncture in the conversation this was probably the wrong thing to say. Meredith shakes her head, gets in the minivan and drives off. That night she doesn't call to say good night like she usually does and I eat dinner alone in silence.

The next day at Custom Critters, I'm talking to an older man who is interested in buying one of my deer heads, when Meredith storms in. She's distraught. Out of breath. Hair in her eyes. And by the look on her face she wants to talk. Now. I turn to look at the man.

"I'm very sorry, but would you mind coming back in a little while? This should only take a moment."

The man, completely bald with ears too large for his head, nods politely and gives me a wrinkled smile as though he understands. But when he leaves, I see him walk toward the parking lot instead of turning left toward the rest of the plaza, and I know he won't return.

"Joey Jr. got suspended from school today," Meredith blurts out as soon as the glass door shuts. She's wearing a red pleather raincoat over her green nurse's uniform. Outside there isn't a cloud in the sky. Meredith, I have learned over the course of our relationship, is always prepared for the worst.

"Shouldn't you be at work?" I ask her.

"He's been suspended for two weeks."

I look at her blankly. Her arms are crossed under her breasts, her face pulled tight. "Don't you even want to know?" she asks. She begins to cry. I put my arms around her, keep them around her when she pushes at me with her elbows, whisper to her that it's alright. It breaks me to see her like this, but I'm also reminded that she's not all barbed wire and brick walls. That sometimes things get to her and it's me that she comes to, that she needs. But I don't ask about Joey. I don't want to. I don't want to hear that he bound some other freshman in duct tape and left him underneath the bleachers, or that he held down a frail, studious kid while a group of jocks doused him in urine. What Meredith doesn't understand is that I won't sympathize with Joey. I'll champion the case of whoever it is he's wronged because I still remember what it was like trying to hold back tears in front of a locker room full of boys.

I rub Meredith's back. She continues to cry, and finally, I give in.

"What did he do?" I ask. "I mean, what happened?"

"He roundhouse-kicked another boy in the cafeteria. A senior."

I almost slip and call him a prick, but I catch myself. Meredith is upset and I don't feel like talking anyways.

When Meredith calms down, we walk next door to Tom's Diner and order pecan pie and coffee.

"What are you going to do with him?" I ask. The skin around her eyes is puffy and pink. She stares down at her coffee while she stirs it.

"I don't know. I can't just allow him to sit at home and watch television for two weeks."

"What about work?" I ask. "Isn't there some place for him at the hospital?"

Meredith shakes her head.

"Well you should make him work. Work is exactly what that boy needs."

When I say this, Meredith looks up, and I understand immediately what she wants.

"No." I answer the question before it's asked.

"But, Ron," she is already saying, "he could help you in the back and do some cleaning in the showroom. And you wouldn't have to pay him. He could work for free. As punishment."

"Punishment for who?" I ask. But I know that arguing is pointless. Like volunteering at the dojo, Meredith is already lifting my arm for me.

"I'll drop him off tomorrow at seven," she says, "on my way to work." She leans across the lime-colored tabletop and kisses me.

"I have to get back to the hospital," she says. "Denise is covering my shift."

For the first two days, Joey and I don't speak more than two words at a time to each other. "Don't touch." "I won't." "Lunch time." "Not hungry." "Go home." "I wish."

We're the opposing parties of an unsuccessful duel, forced to serve our sentences together. Joey sits behind the counter in the showroom, and I spend as much time in my workshop as I can: cleaning, organizing my chemicals, doing every task, even the most simple and mundane ones, over and over. Only when a customer walks in do I venture out, unwillingly forcing the two of us to share a room. I want Joey out of my store and back in school so badly I consider calling his principal.

On the third day, I'm in the backroom re-rechecking the inventory of my bird skin degreaser when I hear the tinny ring of the reindeer collar attached to the front door. I walk into the showroom and am greeted by the old man from the other day. He's dressed in orange hunting camo, and he's cradling a stained burlap sack like it contains a fragile gift. He acknowledges Joey with a gray-toothed smile.

"Got something for you here," the man says proudly, hoisting the bag.

I apologize to him for the interruption the other day.

"Not a problem," he says, clearly more interested in showing me the contents of the bag. Behind the counter, Joey is pretending to read a book, but he steals a curious glance at the swollen bag.

"Follow me," I tell the man, leading him into my workshop.

In back, the man sets the bag on the table and pulls it open.

"Gobbler," he says. From the bag's damp interior he carefully lifts out a large turkey. "Finest I've ever seen," he says. And indeed it is a beautiful creature. A full-grown tom that weighs in at thirty pounds when I place it on the scale. The bird's chest is wide and full, the wattle stretching along its throat like a scarlet ribbon. A bristly beard, at least a half a foot long, hangs from its upper chest, and the bird's feathers are a burnished gold.

"Got him out by Walnut Creek," the man says. "I'd been waiting in my blind all morning without seeing a thing when he came strutting by." His face is wrinkled with excitement. "I want to have him mounted for my son. He's coming in from Cincinnati in a few weeks." He nods toward the front of the store. "That your boy out there?"

I look at the man's tan wrinkled face, and think about what Meredith said. *Closest thing to a father figure he has.* The man is waiting for me to answer.

"Not nearly," I say.

When we've made our arrangements, I walk the man, Robert, to the front door. He thanks me and tells me he'll be by next week to see how things are coming along, but that there's no rush. We shake hands and he leaves. When I turn around Joey isn't sitting behind the counter. I find him in the back.

"What are you going to do with this?" he asks.

"Make a sandwich," I say.

He reaches down with one of his stubby fingers and pokes the bird as if to check and make sure it's actually dead.

"Don't touch that."

"I just wanted to see."

"See what?" I ask. "If it was gonna jump up and fly away?"

He twists his face into an expression of disinterest I've never seen him make before, but looks oddly familiar.

"Never mind," he says and begins to walk out. And for some reason, maybe concern that he might complain to Meredith about me, I stop him.

"Joey."

"*What?*"

"Do you want to watch me work?" I instantly feel like a fool for asking. And I half expect a biting sarcastic response, but instead he turns and faces the table without looking up at me. And so I begin to prepare my tools.

For the next hour I work intently. I remove the paper towels Robert stuffed in the bird's mouth to keep blood from soiling the feathers. The turkey hadn't been field dressed so after turning it onto its back, I make a slow careful incision down the chest. I remove the turkey's innards, making sure to point out the heart and gizzard to Joey. The coppery smell of blood mixes with the strong smell of the ammonia I use to clean the workroom. I make a cut on the neck, reach down and gently pull out the sac-like crop, and when I cut it open I show Joey what the tom ate for his last meal, feed corn. I carefully clean away all the blood and dirt and grit until the feathers that remain are spotless. Although the bird was molting, I do my best to begin recreating the feather pattern Mother Nature gave him. Occasionally, as I work, Joey stops me to ask a question. When the time comes to remove the bird's eyes he asks if I will let him take one out. At first I greet this request with caution. If he is clumsy or quick he could damage the socket and make my work more difficult, but I agree and watch as he carefully plucks out the tiny orb with a pair of tweezers. He drops it into the aluminum waste basket beside the table.

"That's fucking gross," he says, smiling. "You do this all the time?"

"Yeah, I have to remove the real thing so I can put in the glass ones," I say. I can tell that he's interested. "You ever gone hunting?" I ask.

"No. I've always wanted to though."

"You should learn," I say. "It's fun." But somehow I can't quite convince myself to offer an invitation. Nothing has changed between us and there is still a question I want to ask him. We are both staring at the turkey, both focusing on the job that is yet to be finished.

"Why did you hurt that boy?"

He looks up at me surprised, but without a trace of shame on his face.

"Because I wanted to," he says defiantly. But he's lying. I tell myself that there has to be more, and I won't allow him to get off that easily.

"Please tell me," I say. I feel that I am owed this, by this boy, by his father. I have wondered for a long time. "What made you?"

Joey lowers his eyes and stares at the turkey propped on its back, listening, it seems, to our conversation. After a few moments of silence, he answers.

"He calls me fat ass," he says. "He told everyone in school that I'm a bastard, that I don't have a father. He calls me the Immaculate Erection." Joey smoothes down a feather on the turkey's wing and then he adds, "Don't tell my mom."

For a moment I think he's lying. But something, maybe the way he hides his face when he tells me, makes me believe him.

"Did you know my dad?" he asks. Meredith, I know, told him once that his father and I went to the same school, but he has never asked me about him before.

"We didn't exactly run in the same circles," I say. I can tell he's disappointed by my answer. "He was a great athlete though, I remember that," I add, even though it hurts to admit it. I wish I could tell him something more, but this is the best I can offer, and I feel traitorous toward myself even for this.

"Sometimes I hate him," he says. "Sometimes I hope he's dead."

When he says this, I see him for the first time as an ally. I want to tell him how many times, in my imagination, his father has died by my own hand, describe to him the look of fear and regret on his father's face when I, for once, am in control. I want to tell him the things his father did, not only to me, but to others, to Meredith. The names she has told me he called her. I want to tell him how, when his father ran off, he left Joey alone in his crib when he was supposed to be the one watching him, something Meredith has sworn she will never reveal to Joey. But instead I say, "Don't hate him." It's the only thing I can think to say. Maybe because I have hated his father enough for the both of us. "I'm sure he had his reasons," I tell him. I put a hand on his shoulder, give it a squeeze. And when I look down at the turkey again, I can see that it's coming together. I'm happy that it already has a home with Robert's son, and won't be one I display at Custom Critters. As much as I'd like to keep all of the animals I preserve, it's better to let some of them go. Looking up, I notice how clean the workroom is. Bottles of chemicals and boxes of supplies line the shelves along the walls. The tubs I use for staining and cleaning are stacked neatly in a corner. The shop is quiet and well-lit and it fills me with something like satisfaction.

"You did alright with the taxidermy," I tell Joey.

"Yeah, well I've been looking at your stuff in the showroom for the last three days and I figured I couldn't do much worse," he says.

"Asshole," I say, but there's a lightness to my voice that I'm sure he can hear.

"Eat me," he says.

Later we meet Meredith at the Chinese buffet on the other end of the strip mall. We sit in a booth and eat shrimp wontons and pork fried rice. Joey Jr. leaves the table to get more spareribs.

"Any progress?" Meredith asks. She knows Joey and I have had a rough start. I shrug. But she can tell. Neither Joey nor I will say it, but the waiter has already brought the check and the fortune cookies and we still haven't insulted each other and that, at least, is something. Joey returns and resumes eating. All around us families are talking and laughing and arguing. Meredith grabs my hand beneath the table and I think of how I might wait awhile before I ask her again to marry me, I might not ask at all if that's what she wants. Just because you're not married doesn't mean you're not in love. Across the table, Joey has a smudge of soy sauce on his cheek and Meredith rubs it away with her free hand. And I can't help to think that somewhere Joey Sr. is missing all of this. That even if he has another family, another life, he's still missing this, the man his son will grow to be, the mother Meredith has already become. And I feel like someone should let him know all about it, about all of the pain and wonder and love he'll miss out on. But I have no desire to be the one to tell him, or even to see the expression on his face when he hears.

The Gambler

IN THE MONTHS FOLLOWING his wife's death, Harold Finkston tried to structure his days in such a way as to keep his mind occupied. Mornings he was up at six, the left side of the bed undisturbed, the cool interiors of his threadbare slippers waiting for him when he swung his feet over the side. There was coffee and eggs, a warm five-minute shower and a shave, the selection from his closet of a button-down shirt, faded khakis, his grayish orthopedic New Balances, a walk to the Saddlewood Patio Homes' Community Center for more coffee and mind-numbing retirement-center gossip, shuffleboard, table tennis, a ham sandwich and chips for lunch, nine holes in the afternoon, one, maybe two Tom Collins afterwards in the clubhouse, dinner alone in front of the TV at five, another shower, rinse, sleep, repeat.

Shortly before she passed away, Edna had convinced Harold that they should move to Saddlewood. They were ready for a simpler life, she'd told him. Harold had recently retired from General Electric where he'd painted diesel locomotives for fifty-one years. Edna was tired of her part-time job at the daycare center. They had worked hard, she explained, had raised two children, watched as those children grew and formed families of their own, and now it was time for something else. They settled on Saddlewood, with its extensive network of curbed sidewalks, its shuffleboard courts, its rec room filled with overstuffed couches and big-screen TVs. And then, two months after their arrival, Harold awoke to find Edna lying still and quiet beside him. It was the quiet he could not get over, a quiet so overwhelming that he'd known even before he felt the coolness of her skin. What followed was to be expected. There was, of course, the grief. Nearly five months after her death, Harold sometimes still reached for Edna in the early hours of morning, followed by fits of sobbing when he found only the soft down of her pillow. His children had stayed with him for the funeral and through the days that ensued, a blur of phone calls and lawyers, sandwich trays and Valium. But they had long since returned to their respective lives: Harold Jr. to his investment banking in Orlando, Carol to her tumultuous marriage to a TV director in the green rolling hills of Burbank. Since that time Harold's grief had changed, thawed into something more manageable. Mostly what remained was a feeling Harold could not quite pinpoint, a clinging unease he occasionally encountered, like stepping into cobwebs.

Harold strongly suspected that part of the problem had to do with change. He sensed it everywhere: at the single place setting at the breakfast nook, in the empty drawers of his dresser, and at Saddlewood itself, a place Harold had been reluctant to move to. Harold and Edna had been married for forty-eight years and in that time had only moved once. It was a reliable sort of life, one that Harold embraced. At G.E. he had been a model employee: never late, never sick, never complaining or arguing with the line boss. Not counting the eighteen months he'd spent aboard the USS *Juneau* during Korea, skirting the emerald waters of the Tsushima Strait, Harold had never missed a day. The other workers joked that if he failed to show, you could be certain he was dead. Harold hadn't been bothered by it. His father had told him to always show up, to do the best with what you were given and the rest would take care of itself. Now, for the first time in his life, Harold felt miserable while doing exactly that.

On Sunday Harold cancelled his tee time with his friend Billy Jenks, a retired ophthamologist, and went instead to the community center's rec room. Artificial light shone down from ceiling units, accentuating the bluish hair of the women assembled at the card table in the corner, playing canasta. Harold walked over to the bulletin board that hung from the cold egg-shell colored wall. The cork was covered with xeroxed flyers announcing garage sales and pottery club meetings. There were take-out menus and business cards as well as pictures of the residents' grandchildren at dance rehearsals and in little league uniforms. A quarter of the board was dedicated to upcoming events and Harold scanned it for any new additions. Near the bottom was a black and white flyer announcing an outing to the newly built Presque Isle Downs and Casino. Harold had heard about the casino, the huge undertaking its construction had been, the polarizing effect it had had on the community. Harold was not a gambler, and had no opinion on the matter. As far as he could recall, he had never set foot inside a casino. Tiny strips had been cut in the bottom of the flyer with the departure time and date printed on each. Harold tore one off and slipped it into his shirt pocket.

The next Tuesday, Harold boarded the Greyhound outside the community center. He waited patiently as the woman in front of him climbed the steps slowly, the varicose veins in the backs of her thighs running like blue and purple circuitry beneath pale skin. He chose an empty row near the rear of the bus and stared out the window at the scenery streaming by. Fallow fields stretching toward the horizon, grain silos and farmhouses in disrepair, sparse sections of woodland on either side of Interstate 90, the naked branches like deep cracks against the granite sky. It was the middle of April. Another long, particularly bad Lake Erie winter had passed. Edna had been gone since Thanksgiving. Harold had briefly considered a move that would place him near one of his children, but hated the idea of himself as a burden. Instead, he did his best to embrace a new life at Saddlewood, preparing Skyline chili dip for potluck dinners, attending scavenger hunts and tango lessons. The facilities were well-maintained and offered constant diversions for which, Harold knew, he ought to be grateful.

It was early afternoon when they arrived at the casino. Harold disembarked with the others and walked into the sprawling marble atrium. The thing that struck him first was the noise. The clanging of bells reverberating from the tightly-spaced rows of slots, the strain of horns from a jazz quartet playing in the bar, the incomprehensible chatter of a hundred conversations going at once. Everywhere, it seemed, there was the steady clinking of coins against metal as machines paid out. To the right of Harold, a woman jumped off a stool and began cheering wildly over the shrieking siren of a jackpot. It was like standing in the midway of a carnival. Puffs of smoke rose into the air from between the rows of slots and hung in a low gray cloud, reminding Harold of the living quarters below deck on the *Juneau,* where he and the other petty officers would gather to smoke and speculate. Harold moved slowly down the wide carpeted walkway. All around him the casino hummed with excitement: a silver Mercedes rotated on a raised platform, a blackjack table erupted in cheers. Harold could feel the hairs on the back of his neck stand up, his pulse quicken. Everywhere he looked there was something to see. When a cocktail waitress in a low-cut shimmering dress approached and asked if he would like a drink, Harold turned to her, his eyes wide, his hands trembling at his sides.

"Is it always like this?" he asked. The waitress scanned the casino floor, the look on her face as disinterested as if she was channel-surfing.

"No," she said. "Today we're a little slow."

Harold returned to the casino every day for the next three weeks. When Saddlewood didn't have a Greyhound chartered, Harold took the city bus, an hour and fifteen minutes each way. He packed his lunch and ate at the casino, chewing his ham sandwich while walking through the rows of slots, learning the difference between progressives and bonus multipliers, memorizing the various sounds each machine made when a jackpot hit. He stood beside the roulette table watching the ball spin in a blur around the polished mahogany of the wheel, silently rooting for the old women in their embroidered sweatshirts, who clutched their pocketbooks to their sides and bet less than everyone else. He learned craps simply by observing, watching while the shooter selected the dice and placed chips on the pass line, other players slowly filling in around the perimeter of the table like boats docking. He met the casino employees, from the pit bosses to the janitors. He memorized their names and faces, their hometowns.

Soon every cocktail waitress there knew how Harold took his complimentary cup of coffee: no cream, two sweeteners, one ice cube. They would spot him approaching the snack bar, cutting a diagonal path through the nickel slots, and by the time he arrived it was there waiting for him. Harold adored this. He would lift the paper cup, nod in appreciation, and take a sip, feeling the gentle click of the ice cube as it tapped against the front of his dentures.

Harold circled the casino floor for hours. People stopped him, mistaking him for an employee. He directed them to specific slots or table games, told them which machines gave the best odds, which dealers were the players' favorites. He would stay until he spotted the last bus that ran to Saddlewood idling outside the casino's main entrance, black clouds sputtering from its exhaust pipe, its running engine causing it to shake like an impatient parent. Through all of it, Harold never bet a dime. Not one pull on a nickel slot, not one hand of Caribbean poker, not one round of keno. For Harold, watching was enough.

Sometimes, after he returned to Saddlewood, he would meet Billy for a drink at the clubhouse. It was usually late by the time he got back and he'd begun to feel slightly guilty about abandoning his friend for the casino.

"You better be careful," Billy said one night over stuffed potato skins and frosted mugs of Yuengling. "You know my cousin Frank in Connecticut lost his entire retirement at Foxwoods. Video poker. The guy never bet a day in his life, and that's what does him in, a cartoon dealer and fifty-cent hands."

They were sitting on the deck of the clubhouse looking out at the eighteenth hole, a long par four, bordered on one side by a pond. It was late and the course was clear of golfers. In the center of the pond, a fountain sprayed a glittering ribbon of water into the air. Near the edge, a father and son took turns casting a line. The setting sun purpled a mountain of clouds above them and threw long shadows across the green carpet of the fairway.

"My cousin sat there morning till night," Billy went on. "Three months of that and he was calling me for handouts."

A warm breeze blew over the deck and lifted a few cocktail napkins from the glass-topped table. Harold watched them go skittering across the grass like wounded birds.

"I don't gamble," Harold said. "I just watch."

Billy lifted his eyebrows. He took a sip of his beer and put the mug back down. "Never?" he asked.

"Not once," Harold said. "Not once in my whole life."

For a few days Harold did his best to ignore the urge to return to the casino. Billy had told him how their other friends at Saddlewood had begun to wonder about him, what he did at that place all day. Harold decided that some time off to keep up appearances wouldn't be a bad idea. In an effort to shorten the day, he tried sleeping later than he had in his entire life, setting his alarm for eight. But still, he woke at six and lay there for two hours, waiting for the alarm before finally rolling out of bed. He returned to the community center where Billy and the others welcomed him back with open arms, penciling his name onto the shuffleboard schedule, challenging him to games of table tennis, catching him up on all the gossip he'd missed. Mr. Hammel was going to need another stent placed in his heart. Kate Sewickley's granddaughter was expecting twins. Someone had stolen a case of bottled water from the community center's supply closet, inquiries were being made. Harold nodded along, listening with feigned interest as Billy and the others brought him up to speed. All the while his mind roared with the clang of slots, the explosive cheer of a blackjack table after a dealer's bust, all the never-ending noise and risk and excitement that was undoubtedly still taking place without him.

Two weeks later he was back at the casino. At the snack stand a new cocktail waitress with a short brown bob and crooked teeth listened as he explained how he took his coffee. Harold's heart sank when she slid it across the counter without making eye contact and then went back to typing something into her cellular phone. Harold walked a lap of the gaming floor. The casino looked the same. Crowds still hovered near slots that had just hit, thin streams of smoke still drifted toward the ceiling, people still walked by purposefully, drinks in hand. But it did not feel the same. Harold watched a young woman in a sorority sweatshirt win four hundred dollars playing roulette and he walked away utterly unimpressed. He stood by a noisy craps table where a hot shooter rolled the point number over and over, and he felt nothing. Nobody spoke to him or stopped him for directions. Several of the casino employees were new to him, and even those he recognized gave him little more than a perfunctory hello. It was as though all of the excitement he'd felt at first, the surge of life that had flooded him for those three weeks, had vanished like an ill-advised wager.

In the restroom, Harold rinsed his face with lukewarm water. Dim fluorescent lights illuminated pockets of the room. Harold studied his reflection in the mirror. There had been a time when, although not exactly handsome, Harold had exhibited a kind of youthful glow that Edna called his aura, long before that word was popular. She had always been like that, quirky and upbeat, searching out the best in others. Now Harold's skin looked sallow and loose. His ears, filled with their unmanageable sprays of hair, seemed to have grown, and stood out further from the sides of his head. Behind him one of the stall doors swung open. Harold watched in the mirror as Tommy, a floor manager in the table games area, stepped to the sink beside his.

"Mr. Finkston," Tommy said. "Long time no see."

Harold figured Tommy to be in his late twenties. He was tall with broad shoulders and gelled hair parted down the middle. He wore a whitening tray along his upper row of teeth so that when his mouth was closed his top lip stuck out slightly. Tommy was the only employee Harold disliked. Harold had seen him flirting with female gamblers and patting waitresses on their behinds. He'd also overheard a conversation between two waitresses, one of whom had briefly dated Tommy. She had complained to her friend that after they'd slept together he had stopped calling and now ignored her at work. Everything about Tommy struck Harold as slimy and dishonest.

Tommy pumped the soap dispenser. "I trust that everything's all right," he said, staring at his reflection in the mirror. He was wearing a slim beige suit and a bright pink tie.

Harold coughed into his paper towel. "Yes, fine," he said, "just fine." He forced a smile and picked up the coffee he'd set beside the basin.

"You know, I'm the floor manager," Tommy said, "and it's my job to notice everything." Tommy lathered his hands while looking at Harold in the mirror. "And what I've noticed is that you never place any bets."

Harold shifted his weight. He heard the siren of a slot machine and longed to be out in the casino, anonymous among the gamblers. He felt the heat of his coffee through the thin paper cup. He had the sudden urge to throw it in Tommy's face, turn, and run.

"We offer complimentary lessons for all our table games if it's a question of not knowing how to play."

"I know how to play," Harold said.

Tommy seemed to consider this for a moment. "Then why don't you?"

Harold hesitated before saying, "I just never have. I just like watching."

Tommy dried his hands and smiled. "Fair enough," he said, straightening the silver nametag pinned to his lapel. "But you should try your luck sometime. I think you'd find it pretty exciting." He winked at Harold's reflection as though they'd just shared a secret. "Plus, the coffee and amenities are technically for the players. But I know you're a regular, so enjoy." He patted Harold on the shoulder, and began to walk away. When he reached the door, he stopped. "We also have a whole section of penny and nickel slots," he said, before pushing open the door and disappearing.

Harold threw away his coffee and walked outside thinking of things he should have said if only he'd thought of them in time. Behind the casino, the racetrack that had been under construction all spring was nearly complete. Harold took a seat on the empty bleachers and stared out over the huge oval track. It was midday and the sun was still burning brightly. Across the lush green infield, on the far side of the track, a pair of thoroughbreds kept pace with one another. From the distance he was at, they seemed to be barely moving, the jockeys riding them nothing more than specks of color. The horses made the turn at the northern end of the track. They weren't at full speed, but their hooves still tore into the soft turf, spraying it into the air. The jockeys, in their brightly-colored jerseys and helmets, slowed the horses when they reached the final straightaway. One continued on toward the stable, while the other rode over to a young boy who was waiting near the railing. The horse's body was dark with sweat. The jockey dismounted, handed the reins and whip to the boy without looking at him, and walked away. The boy was slightly taller than the jockey but just as skinny, and wore dirty jeans and sneakers.

Harold walked to the edge of the railing. The boy held the reins and whip in one hand and was brushing the horse's mane with the other, talking softly into the animal's ear in what sounded like Spanish. He did not notice Harold standing there watching him.

"What do you say to him?" Harold asked, folding his hands over the railing. The boy stopped speaking and turned around. Harold saw that he'd been wrong; the face staring back at him was a girl's. Dark eyes above high cheekbones, the thin bridge of a nose, hair the color of coffee, cut short and standing up in places. Smudges of dirt covered her face. She had a serious look to her, as though she was waiting to be insulted, but she was beautiful as well, a secret you could tell she wanted to keep hidden. She looked to be in her twenties. She eyed Harold suspiciously before speaking.

"That's no him, mister," she said, "and whatever I tell her, is between me and Iowa Alice." Her voice was low and carried a heavy accent. Every few moments she ran her fingers through the horse's long black mane.

"That's her name?" Harold asked.

"I should know," the girl said. "I named her."

"It's sort of plain," Harold said.

The girl's lips formed a knowing smile as though she'd just discovered something amusing. "I guess you'd prefer something like Millionaire Maker."

"No," Harold said. "It's just that I thought the names were supposed to be more...exciting."

The girl shook her head. "Oh yeah, what's your name?" Harold hesitated then told her. The girl laughed. "Wow," she said, "exciting." She lifted her hand to her mouth and forced a cough. "Sorry."

"It's alright," Harold said. He extended his hand in the girl's direction. "How about you?"

The girl, still holding the reins, took a step forward. "Nettie," she said, shaking his hand, "from Houston." She smiled as a rush of wind flattened the tall grass of the infield and swept across the track.

"Are you a jockey?"

"First year," she said, "still considered a rookie." Her voice was steady as was her gaze and Harold did his best to return it. "It's sort of an apprenticeship. They call us bug boys." A bucket loader carrying turf rumbled across the infield. Nettie looked absently in the direction of the stable and Harold was glad for the momentary break in eye contact. It felt like catching his breath. "The older guys think they know everything about racing."

"Do they know everything?" Harold asked. The girl laughed, a sly smile covering her face. Harold liked the way she smiled, blunt and unapologetic.

"Most of them only know how to make weight, crack a whip, and hover their asses," she said. "Prima donnas if you ask me."

"Do they let you race?"

"Depends on the event, how big the field is. Stuff like that. But I'm racing next Friday. That jockey who was riding her is on retainer for some hotshot owner, which means Iowa Alice is in need of a rider." She patted the horse on its neck. "We're gonna win, too." In the distance, a ring of seagulls twirled above the landfill, their screeches barely audible.

"What makes you so sure?"

"I trained her," the girl said without hesitation. "I've been with her since she was a foal. She's a good horse without me, but no one knows her like I do. Besides, sometimes you just have a feeling. You know what I mean?"

Harold didn't answer, but reached across the railing and ran his fingers down the soft hair of the horse's nose.

"Have you ever ridden?"

Harold shook his head. "My daughter did. She was in the movie business, a stuntwoman." Harold remembered the made-for-TV movie where his daughter had been the stunt double for an actress portraying Calamity Jane. It was one of Carol's first big breaks and he and Edna threw a party for some of their friends when the movie aired. He remembered watching the chase scenes, staring at the woman on horseback in chaps and deerskin gloves, riding along at breakneck speed, unable to believe it was his own daughter. He kept trying to catch a glimpse of her face, as though to prove it to himself. His breath caught in his chest during those action sequences, even though filming had long since ended, his daughter safe somewhere in California. For a long time he felt only pride while watching her chase down a bandit or jump from the roof of a building, but there was jealousy there too.

"Must be an exciting life," Nettie said.

"Was," Harold said. "She doesn't do it anymore. She wanted to quit before she got injured."

"Can't push your luck," Nettie said.

"I wouldn't know," Harold said. The girl studied him and then nodded. Harold looked down and worked his hands against the smooth metal of the railing.

Across the infield the loader raised its bucket, angled it toward the earth, and dumped its load into a waiting truck. The turf made a loud hollow sound when it landed. The horse skittered back, its ears shooting straight up as though on springs. It continued to move backwards, lashing its head from side to side. In one motion, it lowered its head until its nose was almost touching the turf and reared back onto its hind legs. Harold jumped away from the railing. Nettie stood at the horse's side, still holding the reins. For a moment the animal remained like that, stranded somewhere above them, its legs kicking at the air. Nettie yelled something at the animal in Spanish and pulled the reins to one side. The horse came back down, its flank landing parallel to the railing. Nettie snapped the reins toward the ground, lowering the animal's head. "*Calmate*," she said forcefully. She released the pressure on the reins, but the horse kept its head low, as though shamed by her reproach. Harold noticed that through it all, the girl remained completely calm.

"I should get her to her stall," she said. "Too many distractions."

Harold, still shaken, eyed the animal suspiciously. "She's pretty high strung," he said.

"It's in their blood," Nettie said. "A good sign. You wouldn't want to bet on a laid-back racehorse." She pulled the reins softly in the direction of the stable, and began to walk away. "Besides," she called behind her, "I've got enough cool for the both of us."

That night Harold could not sleep. He lay in bed watching the shadows of tree branches play across the wall. He ran his fingers over the slight depressions on the other side of the mattress. The light that came through the open window, dim and watery, reminded him of nights spent walking top-side on the *Juneau* during the war, staring out at the vast sea that surrounded him, moonlight reflecting the crests of waves, the sky, a blanket of stars draped overhead. Harold would light a cigarette and watch the smoke vanish in the cool night air. Beneath him, the hidden machinery of the great ship groaned. It was a noise that was as much a part of his days as the sea, and only when consciously trying could he separate it from the sound of his own breathing. The deck hummed, and beneath that men slept, and all around them was the Sea of Japan, vast and unknowable, darker than any night

Harold had ever experienced. It descended into darkness and harbored dangers Harold could only guess at. He scanned the horizon, waiting for a torpedo boat to emerge, a tiny black point in the distance. He searched the endless sky for MiGs, listening for the steady drone of an engine. All the while he was filled with a great uncertainty, a feeling of lightness that surrounded his heart and raised the flesh on his arms. He would walk to the edge of the ship and lean against its railing until his torso extended over the opaque water. Then he would flick his cigarette out into the dark night, tracing its glowing arc until it disappeared. At those times, his body suspended somewhere between ship and sea, he rarely thought of Edna, or their home, or the life he would return to. Instead, he leaned further over the railing, felt the cool spray of mist cover his face, stretched his arms into the nothingness that surrounded him and thought only of the fact that everything, his days and nights, his life, the lives of the men around him, all of it, was out of his control.

The next Friday, Harold arrived at the casino with five thousand dollars in cash, the track limit, bundled with a rubber band and tucked away in his breast pocket. The bank teller, a woman he'd known for years, had eyed him suspiciously when he handed her his withdrawal slip. Harold was early. There was still an hour till post time and his hands were already moist with sweat. He was wearing gray slacks, his navy sport coat, and a red tweed tie the shape of a rectangle. It was his standard outfit for formal occasions. He hadn't worn it since Edna's funeral. He walked down the main aisle of the casino, the tan carpet sliding away beneath his worn loafers. Beside him, a Bally quarter slot rang as though to announce his arrival, the frenetic flashing of its spinning strobe light piercing the stale casino air and igniting his nerves. Near the video poker pit, he spotted Tommy talking to a pair of middle-aged women in tight jeans and glittery halter tops, who leaned in closely and laughed whenever he spoke. Harold avoided eye contact and kept on walking, splitting the double doors that led to the track and pausing momentarily to let his eyes adjust to the bright afternoon light. The track was already buzzing with anticipation. A group of older men stood in a semicircle near the ticket window, holding their racing forms and smoking thin cigars. Their slacks were mismatched with their sport coats which were worn thin through the elbows. Men and women sat on the bleachers drinking draft beer from plastic cups. A female vendor traversed the assembling crowd selling candy and programs, cigarettes and gum. Some of the jockeys stood near the stalls watching a harness race that had just begun. Harold spotted Nettie standing alone, wearing a bright purple jersey and white breeches. She was leaning forward, dangling her arms over the railing. She looked calm and elegant, like a woman waiting idly for a train. Even from a distance, Harold could tell she was not paying attention to the race. He walked over.

"Are you nervous?" he asked.

"Why? Do I look nervous?"

"You look ready," Harold said. "Do you still have that good feeling?" Nettie looked off to where the harness racers were coming down the home stretch. The sky was cloudless. Harold felt the vibrations of the approaching horses echoing through the earth.

"I do," Nettie said, "stronger now than before." She turned to him and smiled. "You look ready too," she said. Harold slipped his hands into his pockets. A strong breeze played with the flap of his sport coat and lifted his tie. The track announcer read the results of the harness race over the crackly PA system. The other jockeys began to trickle toward the stalls. Nettie lifted her helmet from where it rested.

"Good luck," Harold said.

"Same to you," she said. Almost as an afterthought, she added, "I'm the six horse." Then she joined the others.

Nettie's race was the final one of the night and when it was over Iowa Alice was the winner by half a length. Harold watched as Nettie pumped her fist in the air after crossing the finish line. A blanket of roses was draped over Iowa Alice's flank, and Nettie patted the horse's neck as the other jockeys walked over to congratulate her. Harold sat watching the scraps of discarded tickets blow through the bleachers like confetti, the five thousand dollars still bundled tightly in his breast pocket.

One by one, the jockeys disappeared into the stable, while the spectators slowly trickled into the casino to try their luck there, or out toward the parking lot, eager to call it a night. Harold sat watching all of this, the air cooling around him, his butt growing numb on the steel bleacher. Iowa Alice had been a long shot. The odds had been nine to one. If Harold had bet, he would have won forty-five thousand dollars. Harold sat thinking about this. He thought about it for a long time and it bothered him, but it was not what bothered him most. It was how easy it had been *not* to bet. When he sat down, he had only to remind himself that he knew next to nothing about horse racing, that he'd never even seen a race live. He watched as the other spectators walked to the ticket window and placed their bets, and silently he wished them luck. Then he'd leaned back and laid his hand over the lump of money in his breast pocket. To anyone else, it might have looked like he was clutching his heart.

Harold cut through the casino toward the main exit where he could catch a bus back to Saddlewood. The Friday night crowd bustled around him, searching for open seats at the blackjack tables, waving down cocktail waitresses, moving from one slot machine to the next. Harold felt the silent reproach of all of them, as though each and every one of the casino's occupants knew that he had not bet, that he'd been too scared. A group of college-aged guys in jeans, dress shirts, and ties were walking side by side down the main aisle and Harold stepped aside to get around them. He looked toward the bar near the far wall and saw Nettie sitting alone. The race had ended nearly an hour before and she had changed. She wore a light blue sundress and a white sweater was draped over the back of her barstool. She looked beautiful and anxious. A tall draft beer sat in front of her. She checked her watch and then scanned the casino. Harold slipped behind a faux marble column and stood there watching as Tommy emerged from a cluster of slot machines and walked over to where she sat. Nettie stood up and extended her hand in a business-like fashion. Tommy shook it, then reached inside his jacket and pulled out one of the cellophane-wrapped roses the cocktail waitresses sold on their vending trays. He directed her toward a corner table and motioned for the bartender.

Harold watched for the next hour as the two of them talked and drank. He was seated at a slot machine where he could monitor the whole scene undetected. He felt like a father spying on his daughter, a hidden chaperone. There were all the formalities and signs of a first date. Tommy pulled out her chair for her, leaned in close to talk, twice reached for her hand, only to have her pull it away. Every time Nettie declined one of his advances, Harold smiled. He swiveled slowly on the vinyl stool in front of the slot, stealing glances at the bar when he could. The third time Tommy reached for her hand, Nettie did not resist, and Harold suddenly became aware of his own breathing, shallow and uneven. Tommy tapped the top of Nettie's hand continuously with his index finger as though driving home a point. After a while, he leaned in and whispered something, and then he turned toward the bartender and signaled for the check.

Harold followed at a distance as the two of them walked to the front of the casino. Tommy's car was parked in a reserved spot beside the valet booth. Harold watched from behind the thick glass doors as Tommy helped Nettie in. The cab stand was located at the other end of the entrance. A line of people stood behind a velvet rope waiting. Harold walked past them to an open cab and got in. He heard people complaining. A doorman rapped on the window with his knuckles and reached for the handle, but Harold pushed the lock down quickly. The doorman mouthed some insult that Harold could not make out, and then walked to the next taxi in line.

"Follow that car," Harold said, pointing at the taillights of Tommy's Mazda.

"You can't be serious," the cab driver said without turning around.

"Just do it," Harold said.

For the next twenty minutes Harold rode silently in the middle of the backseat, trying his best to keep Tommy's taillights in sight. Several times he worried they'd lost them, but then they'd pull up behind the Mazda at a stop light and Harold would scoot over and duck behind the driver. They passed through downtown where the bars were noisy and lit up, crowds spilling onto the street. A light rain was falling and tiny drops streaked the windows. Harold had no plan, no idea where they were headed, or what he might say or do when they arrived. Finally the Mazda pulled over in front of a low white duplex.

"Keep going," Harold said, slouching down against the cracked vinyl seat. "Pull over at the end of the block." Harold watched through the rear window as Tommy led Nettie onto the porch and into the townhouse. Harold pulled the bundle from his breast pocket, worked a hundred out from underneath the rubber band, and handed it across the seat to the driver. "You've been a big help," he said, and got out.

He stood there for a moment in the rain, his hands dangling at his sides, puddles forming near his feet. He walked toward the townhouse, quickening his pace as he neared the concrete steps. A thin coating of rain covered his face and he wiped it away. He stood on the porch staring at the red door, the welcome mat, the black plastic mailbox with Tommy's name stenciled on it. Inside there were voices and the sound of laughter. Harold looked down at the doorbell. He tried to discern what was being said, and then, before he could think about it one second longer, he made a fist and pounded on the door. Inside, the laughing stopped. If Tommy answered he would ask for Nettie. He would not budge until he could speak with her. He would tell her about Tommy, the things he had seen and heard. Harold stood there uncertainly. He heard footsteps come thumping across the floorboards, and he waited, not knowing in the slightest what might happen next.

430

ROUTE 430 WAS a weathered run of highway that twisted through Chautauqua County like a long dark river. Roddy Daniels had been driving it so long he knew its turns by heart. This was in Western New York, where the state made its border with Pennsylvania in a sharp right angle. Roddy had lived here his whole life. Sometimes at night he would drive 430 and close his eyes for short stretches at a time, sensing the turns as they came and letting the road lead him.

It was late August and the temperature had dropped suddenly. A dense fog gathered in the banks of the road and lay in patches in the fields. Roddy was concentrating hard, doing his best to keep the Chevy half-ton right of the yellow line when he could make it out, though he'd not seen another car for miles. His wife, Linda, sat beside him, staring out the window. They had driven into town to see a movie. It was a war movie full of loud explosions and young men getting killed. In one scene, a group of soldiers, exhausted from that day's fighting, dug into trenches next to a battlefield where men lay dying. All night long the dying men called names out into the dark. Halfway through the movie, Linda walked out. Roddy followed her wordlessly to the truck and they left. They were already halfway home, the road sliding silently beneath them.

The moon was a quarter full and free of clouds and it made the fog in the fields glow pale. Linda had not said a word since before the movie some two hours earlier.

"The deer will be out tonight," Roddy said. "This cold will have them in the fields." He waited for a response, but Linda only nodded slightly, her long dark hair barely moving as she did.

Roddy grew up in French Creek, a small community several miles from the old farmhouse where he and Linda now lived. He knew the county as well as anyone. As a boy, he walked the woods for hours, studying tracks until he could tell the difference between a yearling doe and a full grown buck, running his fingers along the smooth imprints their bodies left in their earthen beds, still warm from their slumber. He scanned treetops for hawk's nests, and spent entire afternoons watching the shifting pattern sunlight made on the forest floor as it spilled through the crown canopy. When he first started bringing Linda here they took long hikes through these woods and she was amazed at the things he showed her, the shed antlers laying on the ground like forgotten artifacts, the way a perched great horned owl would swivel its head to watch them pass. Linda was from the city and only passed these woods while driving, never stopping to look, or even consider that a world all its own existed somewhere within. Roddy changed all that, hoping that if he showed her that world she would learn to be happy there, away from the city. He taught her everything he knew from an entire boyhood spent stalking those forests. But that was before Linda left and came back, and now Roddy could not remember the last time they'd gone to the woods together.

Two months earlier, on a Wednesday afternoon, Roddy returned home from the lumber yard where he worked as an inventory manager, and found Linda gone. There was no warning, no fight the night before, no phone call at work. Just her half of the closet empty, her suitcase missing from the hutch beneath the stairs, and a note on the counter in her hand asking him not to come looking for her. And so he hadn't, and for a month and a half there was nothing. Until two weeks ago, when he returned home and found her sleeping in bed, the closet full, her suitcase back beneath the stairs. He had not asked her where she'd been or with whom. He was too afraid of the answer, and afraid also, every day when he came home from work, that she would be gone again. Now when he opened the front door and stepped into the foyer, his stomach knotted and churned until he found her reading in the kitchen, or watching television in the den with the sound turned all the way down.

The wind was blowing hard and Roddy could feel it take hold of the truck as though an invisible hand was trying to push them off the road. He gripped the worn steering wheel tightly. Twenty minutes more and they would be home.

"What'd you think of the movie?" Roddy asked, regretting the question immediately.

"It was alright," Linda said, her voice low. "I guess I just didn't feel like a movie tonight." It was Roddy's idea to drive into town, to get out of the house. The silence between them had become an oppression, a heavy blanket that covered everything. He wanted to be somewhere loud. When Linda was gone, he kept the TV going at all hours, and let the clock radio on the nightstand play continuously. The sounds provided comfort, though not much.

"I'm sorry," he said. "I didn't recognize any of the titles."

"It's fine," Linda said.

Roddy followed the soft bank of the road past Clyde Benson's place and then the Holbrook Dairy, with its flat barn parlor where the milking was being done, all lit up with fluorescent lights as though there was a fire within. 430 wound on and they followed it obediently.

"What would you say to a drink?" Roddy asked. "We could stop at Chippers."

Chippers was nothing more than a cinder block roadhouse with a dirt parking lot in back, but there wasn't another bar around for miles.

"How about another night?" Linda said. "Couldn't we stop another night?"

"Alright. We'll save it for another time," Roddy said, and he hoped that they would.

What Roddy loved most about Linda was her unpredictability. Early in their courtship she surprised him at work with a picnic lunch. They found a spot in the pasture that bordered the lumber yard, and when they finished eating Linda pushed him down and climbed above him. She held his head to the earth with her kisses, and they made love there for the first time, hidden in the tall grass not one hundred yards from where he worked. Roddy felt then and for months after, that the stagnant normalcy of his life had been suddenly and intoxicatingly disrupted by a force much stronger than himself. Linda, who took him to meet her friends at a bar and serenaded him with karaoke while he beamed, his cheeks turning as bright red as currants. Linda, who called him one afternoon to help her move, and once the bed of his truck was full, when he asked where he was taking her, gave him directions to his house. Linda, who wore a sun dress and no shoes on their wedding day, whose every arrival and movement was as unexpected as lightning from a clear sky, who in three years never ceased to surprise him. Linda, whose thoughts were as mysterious to him now as a foreign tongue, who somewhere along the way stopped loving him or this place or both since they were the same, and who left him alone for six weeks without so much as a phone call.

430 dipped down between two low-lying pastures where the fog was thicker yet. Roddy followed it cautiously. Soon they would reach the turn off for West Mina Lane, and from there it was a straight shot to the farmhouse, hidden from the road by a stand of hemlocks. Roddy thought of how the rest of the night would go, the ritual of preparing for bed, slowly undressing and then climbing beneath the covers where he would lie next to Linda, perfectly still and silent, aware even of the sound of his own breathing. Thinking of it emptied him out.

They came to a thick pocket of fog, but Roddy knew the road ran straight here and he kept the wheel steady. He turned toward Linda, saw her profile silhouetted against the field that stretched beyond the window. He thought of how arriving home had become the worst part of his day, the uncertainty of walking in and wondering if he would find her there. He wanted to tell her how every moment felt like waiting. "Linda," he said, but she kept staring straight ahead, her eyes focused on something outside.

"Roddy," she said, and when she did the sound of it struck him. It had been so long since she'd said his name. He saw a dark flash from the corner of his eye, then felt a solid thump as the front end of the truck collided with something on the road's shoulder. He hit the brakes and heard the high-pitched squeal of rubber sliding over asphalt. When the truck ground to a halt, Roddy pulled over until the driver's side was clear of the road.

"What the hell was that?" he asked. The bitter odor of burnt rubber filled the truck. Roddy switched on the hazards.

"It came out of the field," Linda said. The startled expression on her face turned angry. "You weren't watching the road."

"I didn't see anything," Roddy said, and Linda turned away.

Cornfields stretched away on either side of the road and the fog had thinned out some. In the distance Roddy could make out the silhouette of a grain silo against the dark night sky. He checked the rearview and saw the road was empty. He put the Chevy in drive and pulled around in a U-turn until they faced the direction they came from. Driving slowly along the shoulder, they went on that way until they saw a dark figure lying on the opposite side of the road. The truck's headlights illuminated the form. It was too small to be a deer. With the headlights still on, Roddy opened the truck's door and stepped out. The cold air bit at his skin. He'd forgotten his fleece at home. He crossed his arms over his chest and walked with his head down against the wind. He heard the passenger door open and then shut and then the sound of Linda walking behind him.

Roddy saw that it was a dog. It lay on the shoulder of the road dying. It was a large brown animal, a male dog, but not of any one distinguishable breed. It was lying on its side, a thick stream of viscous blood running from its mouth. It kept trying to lift its head and when it did, Roddy saw that the ear closest to the pavement had been scraped off. Its front legs were immobile, but its back legs kicked at the air slowly, mechanically, as though they were no longer under the animal's control. The dog's midsection was caved in, the ribs giving way where the truck's bumper struck. The dog did not belong to any of Roddy's neighbors. He'd never seen it before.

"My God," Linda said, startling Roddy. He forgot she was standing behind him. "You weren't looking," she said. "You should have been paying attention."

Roddy knelt down and reached toward the dog and when he did it tried to snap at him, but it was hardly a threat, the animal's jaws opening and closing slowly as it labored for breath. "Easy," Roddy said and laid his hand softly on the dog's side. The animal whined and Roddy lifted his hand. Slowly, and with as much care as he could muster, he parted the matted hair that covered the dog's neck. There was no collar. Blood continued to leak from the dog's mouth, from some injury deep within that Roddy knew could not be mended. He stood and looked at Linda who was crying silently, hugging her chest as she swayed. Even crying she was beautiful, her skin nearly luminescent under the night sky. He looked back at the dying animal.

"You have to *do* something," Linda said. "We can't just leave him like this. He's in *agony*."

Roddy looked at her. *Agony.* In all the time they'd been together, he never heard her use the word, and it sounded strange now. He understood that it existed for her only as an idea, an approximation of pain.

Roddy walked slowly across the road. When he reached the truck he opened the door and the interior light snapped on. Across the roof of the cab, near the rear window, was the gun rack which held the Browning bolt action. Roddy stepped onto the running board, pulled the driver's seat forward and carefully unfastened the rifle from the rack. Once he had it down he laid it across the rear seats. He took a loaded box magazine from his hunting pack and slipped it into the back pocket of his jeans.

Roddy had gone hunting for as long as he could remember. He started as a kid, shooting squirrels and other small game using a hand-me-down .22. For years he went to the camp in Kane where his father and uncles stayed during deer season. Linda never approved and asked only that he not talk about it around her. It became one more thing they did not discuss.

Roddy took the rifle carefully from the rear seats and shut the truck door. He pulled the bolt upward and back and checked the breech which was clear. He lowered the rifle and ran the fingers of his free hand over the smooth finish of the walnut stock. He removed the magazine from his back pocket and clicked it into place below the breech. He pushed the bolt forward and closed it, then slung the worn leather strap over his shoulder and walked back across the road.

The dog was still trying to lift its head. Its eyes rolled loosely and then locked upon Roddy, though the dog seemed not to be staring at him, but at something beyond him. With every breath the dog took, Roddy heard the gurgling of blood. For a moment he stood there looking down, measuring his breaths slowly until they matched those of the dying animal. Linda was still crying. She'd taken a step back from the dog when he returned.

"Why are you *waiting*?" she said between sobs. "Can't you see he's suffering?"

Roddy took the gun from his shoulder and switched off the safety. He pressed the recoil into his shoulder and aimed the barrel at the dog's chest. His breathing was still in rhythm with the dog's and he inhaled and pressed his finger lightly against the trigger. The wind rushed through the adjacent cornfield and passed over them. Roddy looked out over the field where the tall stalks leaned back into place, their ordered rows rising to a low swell at the field's center. Beyond that was the tree line, low and black in the distance. Above it the sky sat bluish-gray and filled with stars. Roddy heard Linda crying behind him, quiet and even. He stopped what he was about to do, lowering the rifle from his shoulder. With the barrel pointed at the ground he turned and took a step toward his wife. Her hands were at her sides. With his free hand he lifted them both, one at a time, and placed the rifle in them. Linda cradled the gun awkwardly, letting the stock slide down into the crook of her elbow while holding the barrel weakly with her other hand.

"Here," Roddy said. "You do it." He walked across the road. When he reached the truck, he climbed into the cab, shut the door, and watched her, waiting to see what she would do.

Eyes Closed

BARS AND POOL HALLS were not places you went to turn your luck. Evan knew this. He was not fiercely realistic, but he was aware there was only one ending to those stories of people who drove to Las Vegas with their last penny in hopes of altering fate. But Evan also knew that occasionally some event, small as it might seem, could take place in a man's life and set off other events, positive in fashion, that might place him on the right track, or at least a better track than the one he was currently traveling. With both of these realizations firmly in place Evan walked into the Gold Crown with six hundred dollars in his pocket, almost all the money he had left in the world, and took a seat at the bar. A few people noted his arrival by nodding at him or mouthing his name silently, and this recognition filled Evan with a swell of pride he'd not felt in some time. It was nice to be known somewhere. Evan removed his wet coat, and set it on the stool beside him. Outside a light hail fell, exploding against the pavement like shattered crystal.

On his way into the bar that night Evan saw a woman being pushed out of a parked car in the Crown's lot. She was crying, struggling to remain inside, but finally the driver, a large man, had her out. Once he did he sped away quickly, the door still half open as he swerved onto Liberty. The woman, who hadn't noticed Evan staring, stopped crying when the car was still in sight, and yelled, "It's a goddamn shame is all." She gathered her purse from where it had fallen and walked off in the opposite direction the car had taken.

Now inside, Evan tried to put the whole ordeal out of his mind. He had more important things to worry about.

The bartender, Thomas, was a wiry man in his fifties. He appeared old and fragmentary behind the high mahogany bar, but Evan had seen him break up fights with the strength of a man twice his size. He was old-school strong with a concrete handshake. Thomas was always indifferent to Evan. He'd bring him a drink or mention to him someone at the end of the bar who might be looking for a game, but that was the extent of it. He never perched himself in front of Evan and talked awhile like he did with the older men.

Evan ordered a Railbender and Thomas brought the beer. Evan rotated his barstool until he was facing the rows of tables behind him. The pool area of the establishment was separated from the bar by a waist-high wooden divider. You had to be over twenty-one to enter the bar, but anyone over eighteen could get a table. The pool room had its own way in as well, a glass door right next to the bar's entrance. It was a Wednesday night and both the pool room and the bar were fairly empty. On the weekends, local college boys brought their dates here. Those were the nights you could make a quick score off some frat boy trying to impress a girl. They rarely played for anything over fifty, but it was fast and painless and you could stay in their good graces if you didn't embarrass them during the payoff, if you made sure to say loud enough for their dates to hear that they were the best player you'd squared off against in weeks. Evan had done it before. He was always sure to be gracious to those types, the ones who knew they were almost certainly giving their money away. He probably got dozens of them laid. The dates loved the daring gambling boys. On weekdays though, it was just an old crowd, the same guys who'd played here for years. They were the ones who knew about the bumpy slate on number fourteen, who always complained about the bad leveling job on the upstairs tables, and who wouldn't go near the Gandy's because of the loose felt in the corners.

These were the men Tonya had warned him about. "In this world there are producers, and there are thinkers," she'd said, "and those shiftless sons of bitches fall into neither category."

Evan took a sip of beer and lit a cigarette. It had been nearly a month since Tonya left, and he still couldn't quit, show her he was changed, or at least changing. She hated him smoking. He promised for a long time to stop, but in the end promising was as far as it got. Tonya was a smart girl and never shied away from telling Evan exactly what was on her mind. "I work, you should work," she'd said, and so he found a job doing late-night snow removal during the harsh Great Lakes winter. Erie sat squarely in the Snowbelt and got piled on regularly. All night Evan listened to his Guns N' Roses and Van Halen tapes, sipping coffee from a thermos Tonya prepared for him while he tore a beat-up S-10, plow down, through endless parking lots and driveways. He formed huge mountains out of the powder that blew in off the lake. That job had been good. He felt like he was building something, even if it was only temporary. Something inside him felt right when he saw those mounds of snow after he finished at a site, but now it was the beginning of spring, Tonya was gone, and most of Evan's mountains were just dirty piles of ice.

Even with a job, Evan still came to the Crown to play. It wasn't always for the money. Although money, winning it anyways, was nice. It was better than getting a paycheck, in the same way that catching a fish was better than buying one at the market. That was just part of it for Evan. He was twenty-six, and had come to places like the Crown since he was eighteen. He liked the idleness of the regulars at the bar, the way his clothes smelled like cigar smoke the next morning when he held them close to his face. He liked knowing that at any time you could come here and choose to place yourself, or at least some part of yourself, on the line.

Evan scanned the rows of tables and saw his friend Jonathan playing in back. Jonathan was in his late thirties and a welder for one of the trucking companies that had a hub down near the lake. He never played for money, and for this reason was a friend to almost all of the Crown's regulars. He had no old beefs, owed nobody, and was in general a subpar player who mainly came to drink and talk. Evan walked over.

"What brings you out on such a lovely night?" Jonathan asked. He smiled, flashing a row of smoke-colored teeth.

"Looking for a game," Evan said.

"I thought you only played weekends."

"Usually," Evan said, "but I'm looking for something a little bigger."

"Got it." Jonathan nodded and lit a cigarette. "Where's Tonya been lately? You never bring her around anymore."

"I don't think you'll be seeing much more of her."

"Oh yeah? Sorry to hear it," Jonathan said. He handed one of the house cues to Evan. It was old and warped, but Evan bent down and lagged the nine ball with it anyway. The first shot of the night always felt right, as though he was just picking up where he left off last time he played. To him, shooting pool was like getting back to a good book he hadn't read in a few days. It was simply the world he preferred.

The cue's tip struck the ball with a gentle thud. Evan watched the ball hit the bottom rail and roll back to almost exactly where he struck it from.

Evan disliked when people asked about Tonya. Especially people at the Crown. He had brought her there only a handful of times, but she was the kind of girl who made an impression, straightforward in everything. The first time they met had been like that. Evan was at Sullivan's, an Irish place near the lake. He was drinking with a friend of his when he felt a tap on his shoulder. When he turned around there was Tonya, a pretty brunette with the slyest smile he'd ever seen, like she knew his deepest secret. She was holding a Jameson neat.

"I don't know if this is how you take your whiskey," she said, handing it to him, "but it's how I drink mine." And that was it. Tonya picked out the songs on the jukebox, and they danced drunken-clumsy for the rest of the night. A month later she moved in.

Jonathan took a cigarette from his pack and handed it to Evan. "So what happened?" he asked.

Evan considered this for a moment. "Same fight as always."

"What fight was that?"

"Coming here. Places like here. She said it shut me off. That I didn't really know her." Evan felt the anger heating the pockets of his cheeks, stealing the luck from his now unsteady hands. "I knew her better than anybody," he said. "I knew her that well."

Jonathan raised his drink. "Here's to bumps in the road," he said. They touched glasses and drank.

Evan listened for a while as Jonathan talked about how things were at the shop. He heard Jonathan describe the falling orders, and his declining hours, but he could not concentrate. He had purposefully neglected to tell Jonathan that when Tonya left she also took her half of the rent money. Evan knew that when he finished talking Jonathan would spread the word that Evan was looking for a game, and he did not want to play with the air of necessity. Jonathan would not tell any of the others, but even he knowing would be too much. The number one rule, the one everybody claimed but few religiously followed, was not that you should always play sober, or always watch your opponent in action before the money was on the table. It was not even to make sure that you were having an on night before you bet, since even the best of players occasionally appeared to be amateurs for no conceivable reason. Pure and simple, it was to only bet what you could afford to lose, and as Evan pinched the tight roll of twenties, solid as a cue between his thumb and forefinger, he knew that the six hundred it made up was nowhere near expendable.

After a while Jonathan walked away. Evan watched him move through the smoky room, dodging players and waitresses effortlessly. Evan walked back to the bar and ordered another Railbender. He glanced down the long wooden surface and saw Augie Mitchell sitting alone at the far end. Augie was a staple at the Crown, a burly man with an expressionless face and a sprout of blackish hair which he combed across the pale expanse of his large pate. In his day, he was a player of formidable talents, but over time it became the drinks he returned for. Evan started coming to the Crown toward the end of Augie's playing days. He watched him once, practicing nine ball alone at a corner table. For a large man he had a remarkably graceful stroke. The cue slid through his thick hairy fingers like a snake through tall grass. Only on the break did he reveal the power that resided in his heavy arms.

He fired the cue ball toward the rack as though it was a cannonball exploding from the side of a battleship. Augie had lost his job as a foreman at the brewery and sold his Harvey Martin cue to a traveling hustler for cash. Evan heard that it got to be that Augie had to be drunk to play, and then he would miss things: shoot at the five when the four was still on the table, rack like he'd never done it before. When he wasn't drunk his hands shook too bad for the long shots, for the delicate ones he'd once been expert at. He couldn't cut or put English on the cue ball the way he once could, and he tore the felt when he tried to jump. It was rumored now that he did collection for a bad element in town, that for a price his services were available to anyone. Evan nodded at him and Augie raised his glass slightly. Since Augie no longer played, they'd never exchanged more than a simple hello.

Evan was almost finished with a third beer when he felt the man standing behind him. He turned and instantly recognized him. He was not a regular, but Evan had seen him in the bar several times drinking or practicing alone at one of the tables.

"You Evan?" he asked. His large eyes darted from Evan's to the ground. The man was pear-shaped with a sizeable stomach and narrow chest. He wore a green sweatshirt with an oil stain on its left side. He leaned on one of the house cues and Evan thought it might suddenly splinter and break under the man's weight. "Jon says you're looking for a game."

Evan nodded and held out his hand.

"I'm Frank." The man smiled uncomfortably as though uneasy with the formalities. "I just got here. I'm back on number seven."

Evan peered over the man's shoulder. Resting on the green felt was the half wooden crate in which the balls were stored. Next to it sat a black leather shoulder-strap case. Evan looked back at the man and noted his sloppy appearance. His hair was a stringy blond nest, and his unshaven face looked almost dirty in the bar's dim light. The Crown had rules on appearance and conduct. Ball caps were to be worn to the front, not backwards or to the side like some of the college kids had taken to doing. Cut offs and ripped clothing weren't allowed, and chewing tobacco was strictly forbidden. But as slovenly as he looked, Frank wasn't in violation of any part of the code.

"I don't know, Frank. You pretty good?"

Frank's uncomfortable smile gave way to an irritated gaze that seemed to fit him much more naturally. "You want to play or not?" he asked, jamming the butt of the cue impatiently into the bar's wooden floor.

Evan smiled. When he played the college boys he let the balls speak for themselves. But when he was facing another player it didn't hurt to work in a jab now and again. A little grind helped you to always seem in control, even when you were down.

"I'll play," Evan said. "Let me grab my cue and I'll meet you."

Evan placed a couple singles on the bar for Thomas and walked through the wooden divider to the back of the pool room. Along the back next to the bathrooms was a wall of lockers. The face of each was only about as large as a postcard, but they were deep enough to fit a two-piece cue taken apart. Evan had rented number thirty-four for years. It was along the bottom row, and he knelt to face it. He entered his combination, twenty-one, three, seventeen, and felt the gentle pop and then resistance as the lock released. He removed his cue. It was a McDermott Sedona made of Birdseye maple. There was a triangle leather tip and sixty-eight inlays made of everything from ebony to oak. Evan bought it about half a year after he and Tonya got started. He managed to save seven hundred dollars and hadn't thought twice about spending it on the Sedona. Tonya wanted him to buy a car.

Evan screwed the ends of the cue together and held it out at arm's length like a sword. He peered down its curved surface and checked its trueness. He twirled it in his hands and admired its smooth finish and rough wrap for grip near its butt.

"How will you get to work?" Tonya asked him after he showed her the cue.

"I'll walk," Evan told her.

"You better watch it, Evan, or you'll be walking your whole life."

Evan still did not own a car, but he wouldn't have traded his cue for anything. It was his prize possession.

Evan walked into the bathroom with the cue and entered the stall. He counted out the six hundred dollars. He would never have played with a penny less than he had. He had lost money before. He had awakened hung over and broke in the morning, unaware for just a moment of what happened the night before, free from the memory as if it was not his. But it always found him, and then he became certain. With his pockets empty he was forced to begin answering all those questions he always so easily ignored: how would he pay the rent and his bills and the numerous friends he owed? It was the same the morning after Tonya left. He awoke, not realizing at first that she was gone, but then, past his cotton mouth and splitting head, it had returned to him, the cursing and packed bags. That morning was worse because for a long time Evan lay in bed and tried with all the truth he could find to convince himself that it was all part of a nightmare, that Tonya was simply at work. Even that was pointless.

Evan patted the money through his jeans. He would never play with just words and promises of funds. Waking up broke was one thing, but there were certain rules for welchers, and Evan knew them well enough to never take the chance. He walked to the sink and splashed his face with cold water. He held out his right hand, his shooting hand, palm down, and watched its stillness. He seemed ready, certain. Tonight he could jump tracks, and as he took his cue from the stall he felt the rhythm of his heart churning steadily within him.

At the table, Frank practiced his draw, trying to leave the cue ball exactly where he desired as if he was some kind of magician. Evan saw that the ten through fifteen balls were still boxed, as he knew they would be. Nine Ball was the only game anyone at the Crown ever played for money.

"So what do you say, Frank," Evan asked, "a race to five for two notes?"

Frank pulled back his cue and studied its joint. It was a nice stick, a vintage Brunswick, and Evan admired its precise inlays. But he could tell Frank was impressed when he laid the McDermott on the table. Frank began to rack the balls.

"Sounds like a plan," he said.

Evan won the break off the lag and took the first and second games easily, but in the third he misjudged a bank and watched the nine ball bounce off the inside point of the side pocket. Frank won the game and pulled ahead in the race three to two before Evan had another chance to shoot. In the sixth game Evan had a chance at a combination shot that could tie things up. The seven was sitting about an inch off the side rail and Evan saw that with a good enough cut he could use it to put in the nine, which was near the edge of the corner pocket. Evan leaned down and eyed the balls over the expanse of green felt. He envisioned an imaginary line, the same line the ball would have to travel for him to make the shot. He straightened up, chalked his cue, and ran his left hand over the white cone of chalk that sat on the divider behind him. It would help the Sedona run smoothly over his coarse skin. Evan leaned down and spread the fingers of his left hand over the table before pulling the felt tightly between them, stretching it slightly from the slate. He placed the end of his cue between the knuckle of his pointer finger and the inside of his thumb. He held the cue as softly as a woman's hand and ran it back and forth over his fingers. The shot was all finesse and Evan watched as the nine dropped smoothly into the far corner pocket. After that the games seemed effortless. In the next one he sank the nine off a rocket break. To win the race he capitalized off a miss by Frank on the three ball. He sank the three through nine, counting each ball as it dropped like a child learning his numbers for the first time. After that they played a double or nothing and Evan won that race as well, five games to one. He could not remember the last time he played so brilliantly, the balls rolling as if they knew and respected him, the cue sliding through his hands like a piston.

In the bar Evan bought two bourbons. He tried not to smile, but when he ordered the drinks, Thomas gave him a slight nod acknowledging his victory. Evan sat down across from Frank at one of the bar's tables and handed him his drink. Frank pushed a sweaty wad of fifties and twenties across the table and Evan pocketed the money without a word. The bills looked as crumpled as Frank. Evan hoped that all four hundred was there but he would not count it until he arrived home.

"You play well," Frank said.

"Thanks. I was on tonight I guess."

"Yeah, well cheers." Frank lifted his glass and hit it recklessly against the side of Evan's. "So how about one more?"

"I just got started on this one," Evan said, raising his glass.

Frank smiled. "I wasn't talking about the drink."

"I know," Evan said, "but it's getting late, and my luck can't last forever."

"That's what I'm counting on," Frank said.

Evan did not want to play again. It had already been a good night. He thought that he might call Tonya, tell her how well he'd played.

"Maybe another time," Evan said. "I'm around."

"I know you are." With that Frank stood from his chair and walked back toward his table.

Evan lifted his cue from where it rested against the wooden divider and walked to the back wall. He began to unscrew the McDermott. When he undid the two-piece cue, the top half slid out of his hand and hit the floor with a crack. He bent down to pick it up, but before he could, Augie stepped over and scooped it from the ground. He held the top half of the cue between his fingers like a toothpick and handed it over.

"It's a beautiful cue," Augie said.

"Thanks," Evan said, surprised by the way the large man spoke. The words came out as nothing more than a whisper, his voice as soft as felt.

"I saw your combo in that one game. That was a nice cut."

Evan nodded. "Maybe we could shoot around some time," he said.

Augie peered down at him. "I don't really play anymore," he said. "I've kind of retired. But I'm sure I'll be seeing you around." He walked back to his seat at the end of the bar.

Evan slipped both halves of his cue into the locker, and shut it.

Outside the hail had turned to a light rain. A warm wind was blowing in off the lake and Evan felt alright walking home. He zipped up his jacket and moved quickly. It was after midnight and the streets were empty. Only a few cars moved slowly past, rolling over the darkened potholes. The air smelled of the thaw, and silvery rivulets streamed in the gutters.

At home he went straight to the kitchen and took Frank's money from his pocket. It was all there: ten crumpled twenties and four fifties. He straightened them against the table top and then added them to his own six hundred dollar roll.

In the living room he left the lights off and took a seat on the couch. He thought again about calling Tonya. He could tell her about his night. About the money. He could tell her that things were looking up. But it was late and the thought of her not answering at all was worse than anything.

His apartment was on the second floor and outside his window a maple branch shook beside a streetlight, throwing shadows onto the dark walls. Evan watched them and remembered a morning shortly after Tonya moved in. It was a Sunday, early, and they had just made love. Outside the sky was beginning to lighten. They were lying together on a mattress in the center of the floor, and Tonya had her head cradled on Evan's chest. They both stared at the ceiling, silent. Evan could not remember now why he said it. Perhaps he felt he should offer her some compliment, show his affection. And so with the day's first light casting shadows above them he told her he loved her eyes, that they were beautiful eyes. Tonya quickly squeezed them shut and brought her face to rest near his.

"What color are they?" she asked.

Evan laughed. "What?"

"You heard me. What color are my eyes?" She smiled and burrowed her face into his neck, hiding from him. Evan tried so hard to think, to place them in some context, to find the answer in a memory. But even with her head on his shoulder and with all the luck in the world, he could never have guessed.

Acknowledgments

Neither this book nor its author would be possible without the care and friendship of so many, too many to name really, which won't, of course, keep me from trying. Unintentional omissions will be repaid with shame and cocktails.

Profound thank yous and never-ending gratitude go to the following:

To Dan Wickett, Steven and Mary Gillis, and Steven Seighman for their hard work and faith. To Matt Bell for his dedication and careful editing. And to the whole extended Dzanc family, for having me.

To the brilliant and nothing-short-of-wonderful Terra Chalberg. Thank you for everything. If Thornton Wilder was right and an incinerator is a writer's best friend, then a talented agent who champions the work of her authors runs a close second, and does so with far more grace.

To all of my friends at Penn State Erie, The Behrend College, for giving me the brief but lasting honor of being part of the finest BFA in Creative Writing program in the country. And especially to George Looney, Tom Noyes, and Greg Morris, gentlemen-scholars and the finest group of cronies a fella could ask for.

To all my family, the Crosses and the Garcias , for keeping me. To my sister for always being there for me, and to her family for their love and open door. To the trillizas and Baby Liz, you stole my heart and I wouldn't have it any other way. And to my mother, una mujer de fe. There aren't enough words so I'll say only this: God blessed me with you.

To everyone at the Sewanee Writers' Conference and our writers' group. To my entire Bread Loaf family, and especially Michael Collier, Jennifer Grotz, Noreen Cargill, Nina McConigley, Ru Freeman, Paul Yoon, Kevin Winchester, Xhenet Aliu, and to Laura van den Berg for her friendship and guidance. And Social Staffers, you know who you are. My idea of heaven is fifteen minutes of drinks on Treman Porch before dinner with each and every one of you.

To Erie, which will always be home. To Merski, Marz, Troy, Shea, Kenny, and the whole Erie crew. To the Deimel family. To everyone from 419 McKee. To Chad Simpson, mi hermano numero uno, and to his lovely and talented wife, Jane. To all the editors who gave my stories a shot, especially Tom Jenks at *Narrative Magazine*, M.M.M. Hayes at *Story Quarterly*, and Jill Meyers at *American Short Fiction*.

To my students, for keeping me busy and inspired, and to all my teachers, especially Cathy Day, Percival Everett, Buddy

Nordan, Michael Byers, and Chuck Kinder, the toughest son of a gun I've ever had the pleasure to know.

To Kevin "Mc" McIlvoy for his close eye, friendship, and continuous joy. To Bill Kirchner for getting me started. To Jeff Martin and Keely Bowers. To all my Chicago friends, especially Kyle Beachy, Cristina Henriquez, and Nami Mun.

And finally, to Kelly, my heart. Always remember, *I'm* the lucky one.